Dedication

For our family and friends

CHASE THE SUN

Sapphire Cay, book 3

RJ SCOTT
MEREDITH RUSSELL

Love Lane Books

Copyright

SAPPHIRE CAY 3

CHASE THE *Sun*

RJ SCOTT & MEREDITH RUSSELL

Chapter One

"You get Dominiq's list?" Dylan asked as he walked with Scott and Lucas toward the *Lady Liberty*.

"Yep." Pulling out Dominiq's shopping list from the back pocket of his cargo shorts, Scott Antonelli then waved it in the air. "I'd be in a heap of trouble if I forget anything," he added. Despite the cook's laid-back Bahamian charm, Dominiq could have a temper on him if anyone dared mess with his ingredients and menu.

The three of them walked to the end of the pier and stopped beside the boat. Scott shifted uncomfortably as Lucas slid his hand in Dylan's. He didn't have a problem with public affection, far from it, it was just there had been a time he and Dylan had, well, they didn't, but he'd thought maybe they could have had something. In fact, he was the first man to get Scott interested in anything more than a quick fuck since…

Not going there.

He distracted himself from the twinge of remembrance

of things he shouldn't think about and the ever-present jealousy in his chest. He had nothing against Lucas. Lucas was damn adorable most of the time and a godsend the rest. The man was good for Dylan. Dylan was a competent boss, but he didn't have the head for figures Lucas did. He wondered how Lucas put up with the state of the shared office. If you knew the men like he did and really looked, you could easily find Lucas's personal space in the room— neat shelves on the far wall stacked with labeled file boxes, a bulletin board propped up and covered in receipts and a constantly updated to-do list.

Scott met Lucas's eyes and then looked at Dylan. Both men stared at him expectantly. "What?" he asked. The two men grinned.

"Everything okay?" Lucas asked. "You seem a little distracted."

He wasn't so much distracted as he had itchy feet. Maybe. There was something stirring inside him, and he wasn't really sure what it was. He hadn't left the Bahamas or the East Coast in nearly three years. Everyone around him seemed to be settling down and pairing off. Dylan had found Lucas, and then four months ago their prissy-pants wedding planner had found his hot and sweaty dream guy too. And then there had been a dozen or so weddings, several honeymoons, and more vacationing couples than Scott cared to think about. It was enough to turn anyone's stomach, all that mushy romance crap. Plus all the longing looks and wandering hands and kissing. *Gah, the kissing.* What he needed was a good fuck. A night of dirty sex and a morning of forgotten names. That would cure him of all these unwanted emotions. He'd learned his lesson a long time ago. He'd fallen completely for someone and learned the hard way that love was for suckers.

"Scott?" Dylan pressed.

He glanced between the two men. Okay, maybe not suckers. Not if you found the right person. Someone you could trust to love you back just as much.

"Sorry," Scott said. "When's Dominiq need all this stuff by?" They had no major events for the next month, and currently the only guests on the island were some rich couple from San Antonio. A stopover in Marsh Harbor might do him some good.

"I can check, but I don't think there's anything urgent." Dylan narrowed his eyes and reached out, resting a hand on Scott's shoulder. "You sure you're okay?"

Scott laughed. Dylan was around the same age as him yet in the last couple of years he had turned into some father figure. Well, more like an older and wiser brother. "I'm fine. If it's okay with you, I won't be back until tomorrow."

"Of course it is," Lucas insisted. Scott smiled. The couple wasn't quite at the finish-each-other's-sentences stage, but always seemed to think the same on any decision.

"Thanks." Scott slipped Dominiq's list back into his pocket and checked he had his wallet. "I'll call if there's a problem with anything." Their supplier at Marsh Harbor had only ever let them down once. Dominiq had not been happy to find there would be no dragon fruit for his so-named dragon fruit cocktail.

He jumped onboard and waited as Dylan untied the line and threw it onto the deck.

"We'll see you tomorrow," Dylan said.

Scott started the engine and slid on his sunglasses.

"And don't go gorging yourself on those fudge sundaes again."

Scott raised an eyebrow and looked curiously at Dylan from over the frames of his shades. Who had told Dylan about Scott's addiction to the cold stuff? It could only be one person—the only one who had experienced Scott falling face first into a sundae as if it were his last-ever dessert.

Jamie. It had to be the ex-Marine who had blurted the facts.

"Jeez, if you can't trust a Marine, who can you trust?" Then he had a horrible thought. Dominiq took the health of all his friends very seriously, and horrors of horrors, what if he knew and decided to put Scott on a diet? An automatic reflex had him sucking in his tummy. "Does Dominiq know?"

Dylan shook his head. "But you should watch yourself. If he catches you eating that processed crap again—"

"Yeah, yeah." He had been scolded once before for daring to eat something not made from the freshest of meat and vegetables. Apparently, burgers, fries, and fudge sundaes were not a food group in themselves and did not cover the required vitamins, minerals, and all that other healthy-balance stuff Dominiq believed in heart and soul.

Deciding what happened at Marsh Harbor stayed at Marsh Harbor, he added a fudge sundae to his mental to-do list. Checking one more time that he had everything, Scott steered away from the pier. He glanced over his shoulder to see Lucas waving and Dylan leaning into his lover. He wasn't normally a guy to get jealous, but he was scarily close to turning Hulk-green. A bar, a drink, and a guy should settle his mood and get these feelings out his system. At least until the next time.

Pushing his sunglasses higher, he then swept his hand back through his dark hair and focused on the landmass in front of him. He had made the trip to Marsh Harbor more times than he cared to remember, but something felt different this time and he wasn't exactly sure why. His morning had been the same as always. He had joined everyone else for breakfast, chatted, laughed, and been given his list of jobs for the day. His first job had been to clean the filter on the pool and test the chemical levels, then he had the hinges on the launderette door to lift, and before heading on his run to Marsh Harbor, he had started the work of replanting the east garden.

Not exactly what he had in mind when he had left Ithaca six years ago, but he had come to accept not everyone got to pick their path—not everyone was destined to get the happy ending they wanted and planned for. Sometimes the direction a person's life went in was his own fault and sometimes it was somebody else's. For Scott it was a bit of both. He'd had his eyes opened and it had been the push he had needed to get out of there. Okay, so maybe his folks had thought it more like he was running away, but that wasn't really it. He'd set his sights on something that had been nothing more than a pipedream. His heart and trust had been broken, and he'd wanted to find a way to fix them. To play out the ultimate cliché of finding himself and a new path. And maybe stop everything from hurting so damn much.

Steering the boat, Scott put the coastline on his port side. He hated it when he got like this. He was Scott Antonelli, free-spirited, easygoing, and fun. Lucas was right. He had been distracted this last week. Maybe it was time to move on for a little while. He could head back to Thailand, Malaysia, or Singapore. His time working at the Singapore Botanic Gardens had been one of the most rewarding of his life so far. He actually was able to use his degree and yet still learn new techniques and discover plants so colorful and exotic, he almost considered them to be alien and from another world.

Singapore.

Leaving was a good idea. He glanced back at Sapphire Cay. Maybe.

MARSH HARBOR WAS BUSY, TEEMING WITH TRADERS AND tourists and captains of any seafaring vessels available. The Bahamian tourist trade was big business, and Scott was slap in the middle of the chaos.

"I'll collect it in the morning," Scott said and handed over the list of foodstuffs to the only stall holder Dominiq trusted in the harbor. "That okay?"

The man behind the stall read over the list and nodded. "No problem," he agreed and slipped the list in his shirt pocket. His smile was all teeth and friendly.

Scott knew everything would be ready for him to collect. The man was an old friend of Dominiq's—Claude,

Scott remembered. "Thanks," he said and handed Claude half the money he had been given as a deposit.

"See you in the morning," Claude said. Then he turned to serve another customer.

"Yeah," Scott said, putting his wallet away. He zipped up his pocket and pulled his green T-shirt down over his ass. He checked the time. Still a little early to start drinking alone. Besides, he wasn't looking to get legless. He just wanted to relax with a couple of beers and some polite conversation. He'd be okay with that. First, he needed to get himself a room, shower, maybe buy himself a decent shirt.

Putting on his shades, he turned on his heel to head for the nearest guest house.

"Sorry," he said when he bumped shoulders with someone.

"Scott."

The heat of familiarity spread through Scott's chest when he heard his name. Slowly, he turned around, fearing he might be right. Could it really be…?

"Adam." The man's name was all Scott managed as he stared into the eyes of his former lover. Adam Ross. It really was him. The only person Scott had ever loved, the same person who had ripped out Scott's heart and stamped it into the ground. Scott blinked twice to check he wasn't imagining things.

Images flashed in his head. Making love, kissing, smiles, betrayal, cops, crime…every single day of their six months together coalesced into one solid wall of fury.

"Hey," Adam said. His mouth curved into a smile and Scott saw red.

Curling his hand into a fist, Scott lashed out, laying a blow to Adam's jaw. The punch was enough to knock Adam backward and off his feet, and he landed on his ass with a painful grunt.

That felt good. Scott shook away the throb of pain from the contact with Adam's face and squeezed his hand open and shut a few times.

"Jesus, Scott," Adam said as he rubbed at his cheek. "What the hell?"

"What the hell?" Scott looked down at Adam and shook his head. "*What the hell?*" Pinching the bridge of his nose, he backed away and looked around at the curious faces of the market crowds.

Great.

"You missed me then?" Adam said cautiously. He sat forward and held out his hand.

Scott considered Adam's hand for a moment. He could feel people's eyes on him, judging him and his actions.

Shit.

Hesitating, he chewed on his lip. This was some massive joke. He'd knocked Adam to the ground, and Adam should stay on the damn ground. Eventually, Adam got the hint that Scott wasn't helping him up, and he scrambled to stand on his own. As Adam dusted down the back of his light-colored pants and composed himself, Scott took the opportunity to look the man over. It seemed in six years not a lot had changed. Adam's eyes still shone all golden brown when he smiled, his jaw was covered in shaped scruff, and his hair stuck up in soft spikes. He looked slimmer, skinnier even, older, but he had the familiar youthful charm in and around his eyes.

Damn, he looks good.

Emotions Scott had buried a long time ago threatened to reemerge—a mixture of hate, love, and regret. Right now, he hated the fact Adam could reawaken that desire, that love, those feelings Scott hadn't had for anyone since him. Not like this. Not the same as he'd felt for Adam. Sure he had said the words to a couple of guys, but there was never anything real behind them. Nothing that meant the relationships would last longer than a couple of months, just enough before the itchy feet kicked in and Scott continued with his traveling.

"What are you doing here?" Scott asked angrily, stepping back to put a little more distance between them.

Adam briefly smiled before he ducked his head and eyed the ground. He seemed nervous. "To the point as always. I missed that."

Scott folded his arms across his broad chest. "Seriously? Do you want me to hit you again?" Yes, he was hostile, but Adam deserved it. Scott still remembered that morning—the cops, the shouting, Adam with one leg out the window.

Adam raised his hands in self-defense. "Not necessary."

For a few seconds Scott just stared. His initial temper had subsided and now sat curled inside him, ready for more fighting. He'd finished with Adam. He didn't need Adam.

I loved him so much.

Calmly, Scott again asked, "Why are you here?" What wicked trick was Fate trying to play on him? Of all the places in the world, Adam was here. Why? How? He narrowed his eyes and looked Adam up and down. He didn't believe in coincidences.

"A guy can't go on vacation?" Adam stretched his neck as he rubbed his jaw again. "That hurt, you know. I didn't think you had it in you."

"You'd be surprised. I'm not the same person from six years ago."

Adam nodded. "Do you want to get a drink?"

Scott huffed a laugh. "You're kidding, right?" So maybe a moment ago he was ready to have a few beers, but now he just wanted to collect Dominiq's ingredients, sort out the liquor order, and get back to Sapphire Cay. He grimaced as he curled his hand into a fist. And get some ice for his damn hand.

Adam worried his lower lip with a tooth. He looked both wary and hopeful. "Thought we could catch up."

"Catch up? With what? Your time behind bars? My time forgetting you?"

"Scott, please—"

"How long were you in?" Scott ignored Adam's soft plea.

Adam stiffened. "Three years." He met Scott's eyes before shying away.

The last time Scott had seen Adam, he was being bundled into the back of a cop car. Despite how he had felt about Adam, he hadn't even been able to bring himself to go to court. He didn't want to see Adam. As far he had been concerned the young man he'd fallen so hard for was a liar and a criminal and he didn't want or need to hear exactly what Adam was guilty of. He read about the case online but he never checked the sentencing.

"So, why are you here?" Scott pressed.

Adam lifted his gaze and had an earnest expression on his face that Scott didn't believe for one minute. "I told you. A vacation."

"And that's it?"

Adam shrugged. "I have some business to deal with first, but yeah, that's it."

"Business?" Scott shook his head. "What this time?" He tried to imagine how bad things might be this time around. "You here to steal from the tourists?" The Bahamas suffered from crime as much as anywhere else. Smuggling was the biggest problem in the Bahamas, what with the many uninhabited islands. Exotic animals? Drugs? People?

"I've changed, Scott." Adam sounded sad and more than a little resigned. Was he looking for sympathy? Scott huffed a sarcastic laugh. What did Adam expect?

"You do remember what happened in Ithaca, right? Your *business* brought the cops to our door."

"That wasn't my fault," Adam claimed instantly. He held up a hand to forestall Scott's talking. "It was a misunderstanding. I didn't do what the cops said I did."

"So you were innocent and they put you away for three years for absolutely no reason. I forgot, everyone in prison is innocent." Scott looked around. Were they really doing this in the middle of the street? People weren't stopping and staring—no one cared the two men were talking loudly in the street.

Scott forged ahead. "You made your choice when you stole that first car. You got involved with all that crap and those men. You got me involved. I had the cops going through my stuff, our stuff. Do you know how that made me feel?"

Fuck. He couldn't do this. Turning around, he shouted to Claude, "Claude, I'll be back in an hour for everything. That a problem?"

Claude looked surprised but shook his head. "One hour."

"I have to go." Scott looked at Adam. "Enjoy your *vacation*," he said and made to leave.

"I'm sorry," Adam called after him. Scott stopped and closed his eyes. Maybe it wouldn't have been so bad if he really hated Adam. Even after six years, there was still a place reserved for only Adam in his heart. "Please, Scott, I truly am sorry. You were never supposed to get involved."

Slowly, Scott turned around. "You don't get it, do you? I loved you. Just being with you involved me in what you were doing. I could have lost everything I'd worked for. I trusted you and you lied to me."

"I didn't lie. I just—"

"Didn't tell me the truth," Scott finished for him.

Adam shook his head. "I'm sorry."

"Me too, sorry I ever met you," Scott snapped. Then he eyed the red patch on Adam's jaw where he had hit him. "I'm not sorry I hit you."

"I deserved it," Adam said softly. He touched the darkening skin with the fingers of one hand.

Scott couldn't stand here any longer. He couldn't bear to be in the proximity of the man he'd lost his heart to. He would hit him again or kiss him or throttle him or hug him. He had to go.

"Goodbye, Adam," he said finally, and walked away.

"I'm staying at the Pelican Landing," Adam shouted. "Room four-oh-eight."

Scott didn't stop this time. He couldn't. Refusing to look back, he headed for the liquor store. Singapore suddenly seemed a hell of a good idea just about now.

Chapter Two

LUCAS FROWNED AT SCOTT AS HE WALKED UP TO HIM. "You're back?"

Scott shrugged as Lucas stated the obvious. He had only just docked a few minutes before and he needed a beer. He'd hoped the bar would be empty but apparently, Lucas and Dylan had the same idea for early evening alcohol and were standing on either side of the Tiki bar, chatting.

"Yeah. Change of plan," Scott said as he slid onto the stool beside Lucas and rested his arms on the edge of the wooden surface. It was a little after six and the sun sat low in the sky, casting a warm orange glow over the pool area.

Dylan and Lucas both stared at him, and it was Lucas who finally broke the silence. "Want a cocktail? Dylan's making us Apple Mojitos."

Scott watched Dylan mix the first drink. It looked disgusting. Evidently, his face showed the doubt he had at going anywhere near the bright green drink.

"They're good," Lucas assured him.

"Sure," Scott said. "Why not?" He'd get to the beer later.

Lucas grinned. "So, how was Marsh Harbor?"

I ran into my ex who spent three of the last six years in prison.

"Same old." He glanced at Lucas, who gave him a curious look. "I haven't unloaded *Liberty* yet."

Dylan slid a drink toward Lucas.

Scott continued, "Was hoping for a hand."

He smirked as Dylan pulled the drink back toward himself, away from Lucas.

"Hey," Lucas half whined.

"After we help Scott," Dylan insisted.

Lucas mumbled something Scott didn't quite make out, but it definitely involved both Scott and Dylan being assholes.

"Fine," Lucas said and jumped down from his stool. "Well, come on," he chivied them to work. "I have cocktails to sip beside the pool. Let's get to it."

Dylan laughed and fell in behind his fiancé, followed quickly by Scott. The couple held hands as they made their way down to the beach and the pier. Scott pushed his hands in his pockets and smiled as Dylan playfully shoved Lucas forward across the sand. He had only ever felt that at ease with one person. One man. His head and his heart were engaged in a war over Adam about what was and what could have been—what still could be.

How could he even think about giving the man a second chance?

Because you loved him, you big idiot. Because when you saw him your instinct was to hold him close and never let him go. Because even now he's still able to grab hold of your heart.

Lucas cried out and Scott stopped, watching the two men run across the sand. Dylan chased Lucas toward the pier, trying to capture him around his waist, only to miss and fall face first in the sand.

He thought on Adam and Ithaca, on Dylan and Lucas and Sapphire Cay, and then on Singapore and moving forward. With a sigh, he started walking again. He needed to work stuff out. What had happened today was a wakeup call. The decision to face any or all of it head on wasn't as easy as he thought. In fact, it was damn hard.

After *Liberty* was unloaded and everything was in the kitchen, it was finally drink time. One Mojito turned into two. The drink numbed the edges and gave him a buzz where his mind was imagining everything was possible. He chased them with beer but when he asked for whisky, Dylan placed a hand over his and stopped him from helping himself.

"What's wrong?" Dylan asked gently.

"Nothing," Scott said. No one needed to know that he was probably in shock. All he needed to do was take the edge off with the alcohol, and life would go back to normal.

Dylan began talking, but he was talking to Lucas, not to Scott. "...the most I've ever seen him drink is two beers..."

His friend's voice sounded distant and there was buzzing in his head that made it difficult to concentrate. Scott blinked and looked from Dylan to Lucas then down to his empty glass. They were talking about him as if he wasn't there, saying he was drunk…or something.

"'M'fine," he said. He deliberately sounded out each vowel in his head but what came out was a slur. "'M'not'fine," he corrected. "'M'drunk."

"What happened when you were mainland?" someone asked. He thought it was Dylan, but he wouldn't bet his life on it.

"'S'Adam," he said. At least the sound of the words in his head were right even if it didn't come out as careful speech.

"Adam who?" Lucas asked. Scott looked over at him, but Lucas wasn't directing the question to him, he was looking at Dylan for the answer. Hell, Dylan didn't know anything about Adam. Why would Scott go mouthing off about someone that screwed with his head and left him feeling angry and lost?

"I don't know anything about an Adam," Dylan answered.

"I'm going in to get coffee for us all," Lucas said quickly. "I'll be back in five."

Dylan came around Scott's side and encouraged Scott to sit on the sand with his back against the wooden bar. He pressed a glass of water into Scott's hand.

"Drink this, it'll dilute the alcohol some."

Scott did as he was told then, and before he felt time pass, Lucas was back and he handed Scott hot black coffee. As it scalded a path down his throat, Scott winced. He was losing the lovely mellow everything-is-fine feeling and was on the way to feeling queasy. He imagined the coffee finding the alcohol in his stomach and threatening it not to come back up. He hoped to hell the alcohol was going to listen.

Lucas sat on his right, Dylan on his left, and he waited for one of them to start talking. They were going to ask him all kinds of deep penetrating questions that he had no answer to.

"You want to talk?" Lucas asked gently. "I can go if you want to talk to Dylan on your own?"

"Dylan's my best friend," Scott said brokenly. "You love him." He knew he wasn't making sense. He was coming down from the alcohol high and things looked bleak. "I love that you love him, and he loves you," he added with a hiccup.

Scott and Dylan had been close for years, ever since Thailand, and Dylan knew all of Scott's secrets bar one. *Adam.* Scott could understand why Lucas suggested Scott talk to Dylan alone, but he assumed Dylan would talk to Lucas later anyway. May as well get it all out in one go. He sipped more coffee and for a long while they sat in silence in a row. Finally, he felt able to speak.

"I was in the last year of college, sitting through finals, working at the botanical gardens for my experience," Scott started. He closed his eyes then moved until he could draw up his knees and rest his head on them. He wondered if the two men would be able to hear him as he mumbled into his legs, then dismissed the worry. He needed to hide when he told this story and they would just have to listen hard.

"I met this guy when I was in my final year at Ithaca. Young, only nineteen, and he was the life and soul of the party. We just clicked in bed. He only had to take his shirt off and I had him pinned to the mattress or a sofa or up against a wall." He groaned as he realized how much information was probably too much. Neither Lucas nor Dylan commented. "His name was Adam."

"He was a sophomore then," Lucas summarized.

Scott snorted. "Hell no. He wasn't in college. Not that he couldn't, he was so damn clever, but he didn't have money…you know what it's like. He worked in Ithaca. I met him at a party, we were together six months." Nausea rolled in his stomach, and he concentrated on his breathing to quell the need to be sick. "We got to the point…" He paused. "No, *I* got to the point where I thought we could see where the future took us." He stopped and lifted his face to the evening breeze. The scent of the sea was as familiar as every other night and it grounded him. "I even thought I was in love with him."

I was in love with him. He was part of me. My future.

Lucas rubbed small circles on his back. "What happened?" he asked.

Scott snorted. "Well, the future didn't happen. That's for sure," he added. "I knew in my bones that there was something not right, but I really, genuinely had fallen in love and I ignored all the signs."

"Was he cheating on you?" This time Dylan asked the question. Scott wished he could say he knew for certain that Adam hadn't cheated on him. That he trusted Adam. But when the cops came and took him, Scott lost the last little piece of trust he had. Instead of answering Dylan's question, he forged ahead with explanation.

He sighed heavily. "I don't know what to tell you. We woke up one morning and there were cops at the door, and when I let them in, Adam was halfway out the window.

They arrested him for stealing cars and selling the parts, and I found out today he was given a three-year prison sentence."

"Fuck, I'm sorry," Dylan offered. He slung his arm over Scott's shoulder and Scott wasn't ashamed to lean in for the comfort.

"You didn't know what he was doing?" Lucas asked.

Trust Lucas to be the one who asked the question that mattered.

"I'd love to tell you, hand on heart, that I didn't know," Scott said. "But I was always suspicious. He'd come to my place late, go out early, sometimes he'd just be lying around playing video games for days. He told me he had a legitimate business that he ran alongside flipping burgers, and that he was going places. At first, I was proud that my nineteen-year-old boyfriend had made himself money and thought that one day he would use it to go to college or… I don't know." Scott shrugged. "Hell, the sex was awesome."

"So you said," Lucas said dryly.

Dylan took his turn to ask a question that Scott struggled with. "What stopped you from finding out more? What is he doing here? Has he tracked you down? Did you ask him what he was doing?"

So many questions Scott wished he had answers to. "I don't know. We had six months, Dylan, that was all. Just half a year of off-the-charts sex and me in my own head imagining a future based on that alone. We weren't much beyond the fucking-every-moment-we-got stage. I'd only allowed myself that single morning to say anything out loud that was anywhere close to commitment."

Scott remembered it clearly.

"How would you like to come traveling with me?" Scott blurted out. *Adam wasn't the type for post-sex talking; he was more the head-under-the-quilt-and-snoring type. Adam turned on his side to face Scott and gave another wide yawn.*

"Traveling where?" Adam asked curiously as he stretched.

"Like how some European students travel after they have their degrees. I think it sounds kinda cool. Singapore, maybe, Australia? I was thinking of starting in Thailand or something like that? We could work our way around." Scott wished he sounded more confident in what he was saying. He and Adam were from different worlds really, and he didn't expect Adam to say yes immediately.

"I have a life here," Adam said softly.

"It wouldn't be for long."

"How long?" Adam asked.

"Most students go for a year. Do some growing up, see the world, find themselves."

Adam snorted a laugh and rolled onto his back. Reaching sideways, he gripped Scott's now-flaccid cock. "I can help you find yourself, baby." He smirked.

"I mean it," Scott insisted. "Take a year out, work our way around the world, well, a bit of it at least, then come back and find somewhere to settle down or something." The last he added casually, as if he didn't care what Adam said next.

"Settle down?" Adam sounded momentarily wistful.

Then he ruined the effect by laughing. "That sounds far too permanent."

"I know you're only nineteen..." Scott started. He wasn't sure how to finish the sentence though.

"Nineteen with a place of my own I pay rent on and income from a good job."

"Doing what exactly?" Scott asked. He swallowed. "You have way more money than just flipping burgers. What is your other business?"

Adam rolled off the bed on his side and pulled on his jeans. "Jesus, Scott. I'm not staying if you're going all bad cop on me."

"Why would you say that?" Scott snapped.

"Fuck you, Scott. I don't have to share anything with you."

"I worry about you, Adam."

Adam pulled his T-shirt over his head and scrubbed at his stubbled face with his hands, then pushed them through his spiky, messed hair. He had temper flashing in his eyes. "Don't worry about me, Brains, I'm doing just fine."

"You don't seem to have anyone. Friends? Family. I've never met anyone. You have money lying around here. I'm not stupid, Adam."

"I never said you were, but this is my life and I don't need you getting involved."

A knock at the door echoed through the small apartment. Someone was pounding the door. Wait. Not pounding. Pushing something at the door.

Adam was scared, his brown eyes wide with sudden fear. He looked terrified and crossed to the window, glancing out at the fire escape.

"Adam, what's wrong?"

Adam didn't answer. He pulled at the catch holding the window shut and tried to lever it upward. He even had a foot out on the sill when the door flew open with force and suddenly everything went to hell. Cops, five, six, two with guns drawn, and Adam was dragged back from the window. One of them was stating Adam's Miranda rights and when Scott could hear over the noise all he picked up was that Adam was being arrested. What for? What did Adam do?

When cuffs clicked around Adam's wrists he didn't struggle. He simply stood absolutely still and refused to meet Scott's eyes. The cops turned to Adam. They were talking at him, something about car theft, parts, cash, laundering, and a cop being shot. Adam was going down and Scott had to stay here and think himself lucky he'd stayed out of it all.

Confusion and noise, then suddenly nothing except the promise that Scott would be called in for questioning if needed.

Standing in his room in shock, Scott could only think one thing.

How could he ever think to love someone he could never really know?

SCOTT PULLED HIMSELF BACK TO THE HERE AND NOW. "Adam told me he did extra *stuff*. That is how he explained it—stuff—finding things people needed and selling them on. I would see rolls of notes sometimes, and I knew something wasn't right. "

"But you never knew what?" Dylan asked carefully.

"Car parts he said. I asked him what kind of car parts? Where did he get them? Why did his customers pay him in cash? All he said was that his customers were rich. I was stupid. Blinded by what I thought was love."

The three men sat quietly for a few minutes, and in that time enough memories whirled inside Scott's head that he couldn't stop the flood of embarrassment that made him groan.

Dylan snapped his fingers. "Wait. Rewind. He was in prison, and he's out, so do you think he is in Marsh Harbor specifically looking for you?"

Scott shuffled uncomfortably on the hardening sand under his butt. "He didn't say and I didn't ask him."

"Then what exactly *did* you talk about then?"

"Less talking, more punching," Scott admitted.

"Jeez," Dylan murmured. Scott glanced at Dylan, whose eyebrows were raised in surprise at the statement. Scott was the last person to get angry, let alone allow temper to have a physical manifestation, and Dylan knew that.

"So, both of you, tell me. What the hell do I do now?"

"Is he still at Marsh Harbor?"

"He said he was. He gave me his room number at the Pelican Landing."

"That's a pit," Dylan said. "Cheap by-the-hour type of bookings."

"Stealing cars can't pay well then," Lucas pointed out.

"He says he's done with that," Scott immediately defended. Then he groaned again and hid his face against Dylan's T-shirt. What was he doing? Defending someone he'd spent so little time with and who he didn't really know. The same boy who'd nearly got Scott arrested.

"You know what you need to do," Dylan started. "You need to sleep on it, and in the morning, you need to get yourself to the Pelican Landing and you need to punch him again." The last he added with a smile obvious in his voice.

"Or you could talk," Lucas said. "Get this all off your chest. See what he wants. Then come back home and drink some more mojitos."

Chapter Three

SCOTT STOOD ON THE CORNER OF TWO UNNAMED BACK roads and stared up at the Pelican Landing Hotel. The 'Pe' and the 'ing' were missing, which shaped an opinion in Scott's mind of exactly how much of a dive the place was. A pit was probably a nice way to describe it. The outside was showing age and needed a good paint job. Dusty windows were full of curling yellowed notices and warnings that had clearly accumulated over some time. Scott knew Lucas was right. He had to know what Adam was here for. So why did it hurt so much just to stand here knowing Adam was inside?

The front door opened and a man stumbled out, considerably worse for wear. Scott recalled just how bad he'd probably looked last night. Thank God for Lucas, Dylan, water, and coffee because he didn't look that way for long and he didn't have a hangover. He was tired but he imagined the cause of that was the fact he hadn't really slept last night and not so much the mojito/beer mix.

He was wavering between anger and nervousness

waiting here. What was Adam going to say? Was he going to attempt to explain? Could Scott begin to listen to excuses? Would Adam beg for a second chance, or basically lie to Scott again? Could Scott keep his emotions in check? He'd imagined meeting Adam on the street somewhere one day and cutting him dead. Showing Adam that what he had done meant nothing. Instead, look what had happened. He was lost the minute he looked into Adam's eyes.

Fuck.

Scott's head spun with the possible scenarios until he nearly turned on his heel and left. What seemed like a good idea last night, to face the old memories, was now less clever. Scott would only have to look at Adam and his soulful amber-brown eyes and he feared he would back down again. Adam had always had that move down to a tee when they were together.

Determining he was going to get nowhere standing here on the road, he had to make a decision. Go? Stay? Resolving he would never know unless he actually spoke to Adam, he strode across to the front door and in a quick motion threw it open. The musty smell of the interior assaulted his nose, and he quickly saw the inside wasn't in any better condition than the outside. This place was a hostel for teenagers on Spring Break packed in twenty to a room, or by-the-hour renters. The cliché no-tell-motel receptionist, an odd-looking guy with wispy hair and yellow teeth, looked up at him as Scott waited at the small window between the bars.

"I'm here visiting a friend," Scott began.

The guy behind the bars looked him up and down

briefly. "Twenty-five an hour, condoms are extra," he said. Then held out his hand.

"No. I have a room number, I need to go up." Why had he even stopped to talk to the creepy guy? He should have just walked past looking like he belonged here.

Creepy-guy eyed Scott suspiciously, then dismissed him with a wave of his hand that Scott took to mean he should just carry on into the bowels of this dark-carpeted place. Four-oh-eight wasn't on the fourth floor, nor on the third. In fact, it was in a corridor off the second floor, and it had taken Scott asking two kids in low-rise jeans to actually find it. He knocked on the door and it opened immediately, as if Adam had been standing there waiting. The bruise beneath his ex-lover's left eye was impressively large, and Scott had a twinge of guilt that he had hurt someone like that. Even if that someone was an asshole who had screwed him over.

"Scott," Adam said in surprise. He shifted a bag from one hand to the other, and Scott looked down to see Adam had a stuffed-full rucksack in his hands.

"So you didn't mean any of it. You're running," Scott snapped angrily. He fought down the disappointment that welled inside him. Typical Adam to disrupt his life then walk out like nothing mattered.

"What?" Adam frowned, then appeared to realize what it looked like. "No, I don't stay here during the day. This is day three in this shithole and I've been propositioned five times, macked on once when I couldn't move fast enough, and have had so many strangers knock on my door I've lost count." He shuddered with distaste. "So I pack my stuff up and take it outside with me. There's a café opposite that's clean. I can watch the main door from there in case you turned up."

Scott forgot that Adam could talk the hind leg off a donkey. Back in the day, his particular brand of humor and life had been a breath of fresh air to twenty-two-year-old Scott bogged down with finals.

"So," Adam said, "you came."

"I did."

"Uhm…coffee?"

Scott moved away and let Adam out, waiting until Adam locked the door. Scott's move was a silent agreement to coffee. One cup of coffee wouldn't hurt. Then he could find out what the hell Adam wanted and what precisely happened six years ago. He could also get his head around why he felt the sudden urge to touch his ex-lover.

Was it merely because he needed to check Adam was really here, or was his libido leading him down a treacherous path? He followed Adam down the stairs and out the front door and inhaled the balmy air deeply. If he had his way, he would never step foot in that hotel again.

The café was a welcome change and instead of choosing a table where they could see the hotel as he had planned, Adam suggested they sit outside overlooking the sea. He looked positively excited about the idea of an ocean view, and Scott wasn't going to argue, he just wanted this over and done with as soon as possible. He didn't care where they sat.

"How are you?" Adam asked as soon as they sat down.

"Why are you here?" Scott countered immediately. He wasn't here to shoot the breeze—he was here for answers.

Adam frowned and the excited light in his eyes dimmed. Scott was not falling for the pathetic puppy routine and hardened his heart against the loss of Adam's smile.

"I came to find you," Adam said.

"How did you know where I was?"

"Simon. I tracked him down from the college records and he told me the two of you still kept in touch."

Simon. Scott should have known. Damn meddling idiot always sticking his nose where he shouldn't. They were best friends at college, and Simon was the person that helped Scott pick up his life and move on to something new.

"Simon wouldn't have told you a thing," Scott said defiantly. Simon knew how Scott felt—had seen Scott's defeat after Adam had gone.

Adam shrugged. "I don't know. He was a nice guy. He didn't ignore me when I tracked him down. Maybe he saw something in me that I was hoping you would see as well."

"Like what?"

"Maybe he saw that I'm not the same person I was before."

"Did you hack into his email or something? Steal his phone?"

Adam narrowed his eyes. "I checked the website for the college and he was listed as an ex-student—he still lives in the same house. I didn't steal anything. I just knocked on his door." He shifted forward in his seat and locked his gaze with Scott's. For a long time they were trapped in a weird kind of stare-off. Adam tilted his head and then sat back in his chair. *What was that all about?*

"I'd kind of forgotten how gorgeous your eyes are," Adam finally offered.

What the fuck? "What?"

"Your eyes, they are stunning. I loved seeing them when you first woke up, all soft and dreamy. The blue in them has a green tint and they are luminous."

Temper snapped inside Scott. What the hell was he doing sitting here listening to Adam wax lyrical about eyes?

"Just tell me why the hell you thought about tracking me down, let alone thinking I would want to talk to you."

"You're here, aren't you?" Adam said after a pause. "I wanted to say sorry to your face. You didn't come to the court, I looked for you. You didn't answer my one call—"

"You used your one call on me?"

"You were the only person I wanted to see. Then you didn't visit me in prison, so I never got the chance to tell you how sorry I was."

"Court? Prison? You were nothing to me, Adam Ross, just six months of good sex punctuated with lies."

"I could have explained—"

"Explained what? You had your leg out the window and the cops were in the room. Accusing me of the same shit you had pulled. How were you going to explain that away?"

"I was young," Adam said gently. He held up a hand when Scott made as if to talk. "It's no excuse, but that was almost six years ago. I broke the law, I did my time, I worked several places inside, including the kitchens, found what I was good at. I'm at college now, with a sponsored scholarship."

"College?"

Adam looked down and away at this, and Scott immediately thought Adam was lying again, but then he looked up at Scott and there was embarrassment on his face.

"Nothing fancy like you. Just at culinary school. But I'm good with food, and one day I'll have my own place and you'll come visit it and see I've done well." Adam sounded proud, sliding toward defiant—like he expected Scott to laugh. Suddenly, this was all too much. Scott didn't want to be here. He stood and Adam immediately copied.

"So, you're at college, you're well," he summarized. "I guess you just need to add the sorry part and I can go."

"You're going already?" Adam looked down at the mug of coffee that was still steaming. "I thought we could talk more," he added a little desperately.

"Just the sorry is fine," Scott said.

"Well, I am sorry." Adam nodded. "I was sorry the day you saw me get dragged out of your room. I was sorry that I couldn't lie next to you in bed and agree to go traveling. I'm sorry we met at the party where I was cutting deals. I'm sorry I was stupid enough to think easy money meant an easy life. I'm sorry, okay?" Adam's voice had grown louder with each apology, and his voice was choked with emotion.

This was dangerous. Scott wanted to reach over the table and hug Adam. He looked so broken and desperate for Scott to forgive him, or at least to understand what had happened. Scott could try and kid himself that after six years he was over Adam. But he wasn't. That much was clear. Risky. Scott had to push Adam away before he opened himself up to a possible future only to have it ripped away.

"You're forgiven," Scott said in his best offhand way. The words cut deep, judging by the grief-stricken expression on Adam's face. "I need to go."

Without looking back, he returned to the road and back to where the *Lady Liberty* was tied up.

He needed to get away from Adam before he just turned around and shook the brat silly. They could have had so much. And it had all gone to shit.

He didn't even look back as *Liberty* edged out into calm blue waters. He couldn't face looking back and seeing Adam at all. That was the best way. Then his heart could stay intact.

Chapter Four

WELL, THAT HURT. HE DIDN'T BLAME SCOTT FOR NOT wanting to listen. He really didn't. Hell, he'd probably be just as pissed if someone had treated him the way he had treated Scott. At nineteen years old, he'd felt on top of the world and really thought he had it all and nothing would ever touch him. But then he'd gotten himself mixed up in some serious stuff and the proverbial shit had well and truly hit the fan.

Adam sat in his seat and stared at his coffee. He felt deflated, though he wasn't sure what he had expected to happen. It wasn't as if he had fooled himself into believing Scott would welcome him back with open arms and they'd pick right on up from where they'd left off. But he had really hoped to see a glimmer of something. Something to hold onto that meant the last six years hadn't been a waste of his time and maybe someone—Scott—gave a damn about him. He sipped at his coffee and gazed at the couple sitting at the neighboring table. They were clearly tourists as they excitedly discussed their plans for the day, holding onto one another's hands above the table.

He remembered back to the wistful conversations in bed between him and Scott. Plans to travel together, to settle down, to have a future as a couple. He'd never taken it seriously, and for that he was sorry. He'd let the one honest and pure thing in his life slip through his fingers. His own pride and stupidity had led to him losing the man he dared to call lover.

I love you. The words he could never have said. Not back then. But three years in the company of liars, cheats, and thugs, he suddenly realized how good he'd had it. He knew Scott had gotten attached far more quickly than he had, and Scott's suggestion of moving beyond the six months of mind-blowing sex and into the realm of *official* had left him running scared. He just wished he'd had the chance to run right on back and into Scott's bed. Prison had been a place for thinking, and he'd done more than he cared for. He'd looked around and seen exactly where he was heading, and it had left a bitter taste.

What if? That's what it came down to in the end. All those possibilities and this is where he ended up.

He'd been bussing tables for the last two years, saving everything he could in the hope one day he would find Scott. The man had gotten under his skin and in his heart more than he had ever dared to admit in their time together. It had hurt Scott hadn't visited him inside, and all he could think about was making things right between them when he got out. Just to say sorry.

His cell phone rang and he quickly fished it out of the

front his bag. He stared at the name on the screen and shook his head.

"Not now," he whispered to himself, canceling the call. This was supposed to be a fresh start. A chance to do things right. A beat and his cell was ringing again. He chose to ignore it, instead focusing his attention on the pattern on the side of his coffee cup.

Just give it up. His cell stopped ringing, but quickly started all over again. He looked from his phone to the couple. The woman gave him a quizzical look. She probably thought it odd him ignoring his phone.

"Damn it," he hissed and answered the call. "Bobby," he said. He stood, picked up his bag, and headed in search of somewhere more private. "What do you want?"

"Thought you were ignoring me," Bobby Norton replied.

"I was," Adam said bluntly. He held his cell tightly as he swerved between people in the street.

"Don't be like that."

Don't be like that? Was he serious? Adam sniffed a laugh as he thought on how Scott must have felt about a face from the past turning up in his life again after so many years. "Maury said you were out of prison."

"Yeah, I'm on his couch. He said you'd gone to college. Cooking?"

Adam cleared his throat, relaxing a little as the people thinned out and he stood at the edge of the pier. He looked down at the water and then out across the ocean. Scott was out there somewhere.

"Adam?"

"Yeah," he said. "Yeah, college." Maury shouldn't have said anything. The three of them had been friends for years—him and the twins, Maury and Bobby. They were a year ahead of him at school, and Adam's mom had always said the older boys were nothing but trouble and a bad influence. She'd been right.

"Cooking. Like that Ramsay guy on TV?"

"I guess." Adam pursed his lips. He should never have agreed to swapping numbers. But Maury had had that look he used that never failed to get Adam to do what he was asked. The one where Adam could do nothing to resist the pleading stare as Maury asked him to help Bobby. Maury thought his brother could be saved. Adam had changed his life, maybe Bobby could too.

He wanted to end the call but he'd promised Maury that he would tell him if Bobby contacted Maury. He had to play along and find out what Bobby was up to.

At eighteen years old, Maury's life had done a complete one-eighty when he had gotten a girl pregnant and suddenly had to be a responsible adult. Bobby's life, on the other hand, had been a straight line to prison, and he'd taken Adam along for the ride. At the time, Adam would have followed Bobby anywhere and hell if he didn't reap the rewards. He just hadn't realized, or more likely hadn't wanted to see, exactly how deep Bobby was in. For fuck's sake, that last time, the idiot had brought a gun with him. Guns! Adam didn't do guns. What he did hadn't hurt anyone, or at least that's what he thought back then. As it was, it had been nothing but an omen as everything went pear-shaped and some undercover cop had taken a bullet in the foot. Luckily, that part of it had been pinned on Bobby, and Bobby was the one who got the extra two years.

"What do you want, Bobby?" Adam asked and lowered his bag to the ground. "I'm kind of in the middle of something."

Bobby continued, "I was hoping we could hook up. Talk business. It's been a while."

Business? He had done his best to stay away from Bobby's kind of *business* for two years. Sure, it had been hard. He missed the excitement, the money, the ease of slipping into bad habits. He was good with food, but learning the marketable skills was a long process. Added to which he had a record now. Who was going to hire him? As to getting his own place? That was going to be damn hard and sometimes he wanted to curl into a ball and scream and shout and just give up. Being *bad* was easier. But he never wanted to go back inside. Not ever again.

Closing his eyes, he said firmly, "I can't. I don't do that anymore."

"You've gone soft," Bobby said.

Adam chewed on the inside of his mouth. "More like seen sense." He opened his eyes and stepped forward, looking down at the water.

Bobby laughed. "I didn't realize learning how to flip burgers in a greasy joint paid so well."

Money, it was always about money. From having everything, he was now only just getting by working two jobs, attending college, and renting a room off a friend. "What's the job?" he asked. There was no harm in asking, right? He could imagine Bobby smiling on the other end of the phone.

"We should talk over a beer."

Shit. He shouldn't have even mentioned it. Why did he even do that? He was such an idiot. "Look. Maybe another time, yeah?" He had to figure out what he was going to do. Was he going to stay in the Bahamas and persuade Scott to give him another chance? Or was it time to head home with his tail between his legs?

"Sure," Bobby said. "I'll be in touch."

Adam hung up and slipped his phone into his back pocket. He tried to decide which was the bigger mistake— Scott or Bobby? At least he knew how to be the man Bobby needed. He wasn't sure if he could ever live up to the man Scott needed him to be.

His mind was elsewhere and he should have been paying attention. "Hey!" he yelled as someone bumped into him and his bag was grabbed. Regaining his balance, he ran after the youth who had stolen his bag.

You have got to be kidding me.

The thief was just a kid, a teenager.

"Get back here," he called and gave chase.

Shit me. The kid was fast and Adam struggled to keep up as the youngster used his local knowledge and darted between two buildings. Adam followed. All his belongings were inside his bag—his passport, his money. He ran as fast as he could, but the kid was faster and Adam watched hopelessly as the boy swiftly turned another corner.

Fuck. Head down, he rushed after him and swung around the edge of the building. Clumsily taking the corner, he skidded and tripped. With a grunt, he hit the side of the brick building, pain sparking in his temple as he slid to the floor. He landed on his ass with a bump and coughed as a cloud of dirt shot into the air around him. He leaned back against the wall and stared down the narrow street. The boy and his bag were nowhere in sight.

Well, this was just great. He grimaced as he touched his split brow. He was bleeding. Perfect. Fucking perfect. He sat on the floor and held his head in his hands. What the hell was he going to do?

AN HOUR AT THE POLICE STATION AND ADAM WAS CLOSE to losing it. He was tired of being looked at like he was an idiot, like it was his fault, like he should have run that little bit faster.

"I have to go all the way to Nassau to get a replacement passport?" Adam said. How the hell was he going to get to the next island? He had no money. "Can I not fill out a form here? Can you not fax it over to them or something?"

The police officer's face was expressionless as he stared at Adam across the counter. "You need to visit the US Embassy in person. Opening times are Monday 9am to 11am then 1pm to 3pm, Wednesday—"

"Yes, you said that already," Adam said. Apparently, he now had a three-day wait for help.

"Would you like me to write it down?" The officer picked up pen and paper and began to write down the times.

"Can I just borrow a computer and print it off?"

"I'm sorry, computers are for official access only. I am covering evening and don't have access to the system."

"What if you have an emergency?"

"You think you are an emergency?"

"I'm stranded in the Bahamas," Adam pointed out. The officer simply raised an eyebrow. The obvious implication was that everyone wished they were so lucky.

Adam bit back the comment he wanted to make and instead remained polite. "Thanks for your help," he said and snatched the paperwork off the desk. He needed some air and a moment to calm down. The US Embassy was in Nassau and with no ID, no money, and no airline ticket to show he needed to get back, he was looking at two weeks or longer to get a replacement passport. He'd been informed, however, if he could get to the embassy, he might get some kind of loan off them to tide him over, depending on their funds.

He stepped outside into the sunlight. He needed to call the bank and cancel his cards and then call his mom and hope she could get a copy of his birth certificate out to him. He wondered if she could wire him some money. *Shit*. She wouldn't have any money. His family didn't have money. He had nowhere to stay. Nothing to pay for another night. Clutching his chest, he took deep breaths. Fuck, he felt like he was having a heart attack. *Calm down. Calm the fuck down.*

Okay, first thing he needed to cancel everything. He frowned. Like he even knew who to call. He needed to get online and look it up. So, problem number one, he had no internet access. His wages were spent on food and rent and saving to come out here, not the latest smartphone. He pulled the old Nokia out his back pocket and checked the screen. Problem two, no charger for his bastard phone. He still had three-quarters of the battery bar, but that wouldn't last long if he had to call home.

He chewed on his lip. There was only one real option right now. He needed a boat to get to Nassau, somewhere to stay, a change of clothes, and the use of a phone and the internet.

Crap. He scrolled through his contacts and stared at the one number that might be of some use. Sapphire Cay. He'd taken the number off the website he'd found for the island. He hadn't lied to Scott before, Simon had helped him out, or rather, pointed him in the right direction. Sapphire Cay looked amazing from the pictures he'd found online, a paradise.

Would Scott even care that Adam was in trouble? It wasn't as if he had any other option.

Hesitantly, he held his thumb over the call button. He wasn't sure he could take Scott rejecting his plea for help.

"Be brave," he said out loud. Nodding, he took a deep breath as he psyched himself up. Here went nothing. His mouth went dry and he swallowed awkwardly as he hit dial. It felt like an eternity, but eventually a man answered.

"Sapphire Cay, Lucas speaking."

"Hi," Adam said. "Erm." What was he supposed to say?

"Hi. Can you hold on a moment?"

"Erm, sure." Adam waited, listening as there was a strange collection of sounds.

"Sorry about that." Lucas cleared his throat. "So, what can I do for you?"

Adam hesitated.

"Hello?"

"Sorry." He could do this. He could ask for help. "Is Scott there, please?"

"Sure."

"Tell him it's Adam."

Chapter Five

SCOTT SAT AT DYLAN'S DESK AND STARED AT THE receiver lying on its side next to a stapler. Adam. Inhaling and exhaling noisily, he cleared his throat then picked up the phone.

"Adam?" he began.

"Hi, I'm really sorry to do this…" Adam stopped and Scott waited for more. "I had my bag stolen."

Scott sat back in the chair. That kind of thing happened all the time in tourist season, what did Adam want Scott to do about it?

"And?" he asked.

"And everything is gone, my money, my passport." He stopped again. Scott listened hard and it sounded like Adam was near to tears. "I fell into a wall."

"Are you okay?" Scott asked instinctively. He immediately regretted saying a word. Showing concern betrayed him and left him vulnerable.

"I'll be fine. I have to go to Nassau on Monday to get everything sorted out."

"Okay."

Silence.

"I don't have any money," Adam admitted miserably.

"None at all?"

"Twenty-four dollars."

"You mean you had all your money in your bag." *How stupid can you be?*

"And my passport, return ticket, my clothes. All I have is my cell phone and what I am wearing now. Everything else is gone…" Adam fell silent again and Scott considered what to say. His bruised heart had him already on a boat going to rescue Adam; his head, though, was having different ideas. How did he know Adam was even telling the truth?

"Are you telling me the truth?" Scott asked finally.

"It's okay," Adam responded. "I shouldn't have bothered you. I'm sorry."

Scott got the sense Adam was going to end the damn call. Abruptly, his heart won out. "I'll be there soon."

"I'll pay you back, I only need enough for three nights and a trip to Nassau, then the embassy will float me a loan—"

Scott interrupted the flow of Adam's relief-filled words. "Go to the dock, I'll be there in an hour." Then he ended the call.

Scott stepped out of the office and instantly wished he'd stayed hidden away when he found Lucas and Dylan waiting in the corridor.

"Well?" Dylan asked. "What did he want?"

If only the alcohol hadn't loosened his tongue as much as it had last night. He had said far too much about Adam.

"He's been mugged, lost everything. I'm going to go fetch him."

"What?" Lucas said. He had a look. One that said he was not happy about a convicted criminal coming to the island, his and Dylan's home.

"He got his things stolen," Scott informed them. "His bag and everything in it. Passport, money, tickets."

"Is he okay?" Dylan looked more concerned about Adam's situation than him coming to the island. Lucas looked a little guilty.

Scott nodded. "Apart from having no money and no way to get to the embassy and nowhere to stay, yeah, he's fine. I know it's short notice, but could he maybe stay here? He can share with me."

"You really want that?" Lucas asked, bemused. "You can't share with him if you have all this baggage. You trust him?" That was evidently the important question that Lucas needed an answer to.

"I'll keep him on a short leash," Scott finally said. It was all he could say at the end of the day.

Apparently, that was enough for Lucas. "I'll go make sure one of the empty staff cabins is free of bugs." Scott watched him walk away and pressed his lips in a line. He felt as uneasy as Lucas had looked.

"Don't mind him." Dylan smiled comfortingly. "You okay about it?"

Scott wasn't sure. "Adam never found it easy to ask for help. He never talked about his feelings. Anything too serious he turned it into some kind of joke." He folded his arms across his chest. "I really thought this morning was going to be goodbye and the end of it. I'd made peace with the idea."

"Made peace?" Dylan sighed and shook his head. "You shouldn't have to make peace about your feelings."

"I'm not sure I can go through all that crap again."

Dylan pursed his mouth and curled down his bottom lip as he looked thoughtfully at Scott. "Do you believe he's changed? Do you believe he *can* change?"

Shrugging, Scott said, "I don't know. Maybe. Yeah, I guess everyone deserves to be listened to."

"People *do* make mistakes."

Scott sniffed a laugh. "Yeah. Like they forget to pick up the dry cleaning. He went to prison. He lied to me for six months about what he was doing, who his friends were. And let's face it, I let him lie to me. I damn well knew something was wrong. But I was so blinded by how perfect this thing was between us, I didn't want to see it." He looked at Dylan, who looked right back. "I should go."

"Have you thought about taking him straight to Nassau?"

"I considered it." Scott sighed "I don't know what the hell is in my head—I just can't abandon him."

"Seems to make sense to me," Dylan replied. "If he doesn't need to get to the embassy until Monday and given that we need the *Liberty* to ferry the supplies tomorrow, you may as well bring him here. So don't go second-guessing yourself."

"Are you really sure it's okay to bring him here? I can get him a room somewhere, loan him some money for clothes or whatever."

Dylan stepped forward and rested his hand on Scott's

shoulder. "He's welcome here if you need somewhere to straighten this out. You know that."

"But Lucas…"

"Leave Lucas to me," Dylan reassured him.

"Okay." He knew Lucas didn't mean anything by it; the man just liked things to be perfect. Despite the idyllic setting, there were still a lot of things to do on the business side, and he knew Dylan had to make Lucas step back from it all now and again.

"Just keep Adam to this side of the island and away from the guests. They leave on Tuesday."

Scott nodded. As far as he was aware, Adam was a car thief—*had been a car thief*—and didn't go snooping in people's bedrooms and riffling through their things for Rolexes or diamond necklaces. "Not a problem."

"Come find us when you get back and we'll help get him settled."

"Thanks. I promise to keep an eye on him."

Dylan smiled. "Sure. But you never know, he might surprise you and be the paragon of virtue."

Scott leaned against the doorframe as Dylan walked away. He breathed in deeply and ran a hand back through his hair. Dylan was right, he figured. Perhaps Adam had changed enough that he and Scott could be friends. Even after everything—the pain, the regrets—he still had affection for the friend he had made. He shouldn't just accept that he had to move on. There were such things as second chances. Pushing off the frame, he headed to reception and outside. Though he didn't want to admit it, he was scared.

Mostly scared to listen to whatever else Adam had to

say, because what if all it caused was more heartache and disappointment? What if he believed Adam and opened up his heart to the guy only to have it stomped on? He rubbed at his chest as he headed out onto the sand. His heart wasn't ready to be broken again. But then, he wasn't some loved-up college kid anymore, and he wouldn't be treated like an idiot. Nor would he let anything slide. He wanted to confront everything and not stop himself asking questions for fear Adam would run off.

Then again, on Sapphire Cay, where was Adam going to run?

Scott reached the pier and untied the line before jumping on board. Maybe Dylan was right and Adam would surprise him. He smiled to himself as he started the engine. After all, he did like surprises. Normally.

Finals were a drag. That was Scott's official take on them. Closing his eyes, he lifted his face to the sky and felt the warmth of the sun on his cheeks. What he wouldn't give for a cold beer right about now. With a sigh, he opened his eyes and shifted his position to sit cross-legged on the blanket. He'd been stuck indoors for days and needed the fresh air. Hopefully, it would renew his enthusiasm for note making and cue cards.

" 'S'up," someone said cheerfully from above him.

Scott looked up and smiled. "Hey," he said and patted the space beside him on the blanket. "What are you doing here?"

Adam sat down, crossing his legs as he leaned back. "Shift doesn't start for an hour. Thought I'd see how my favorite student was doing." Adam rolled his head as he met Scott's eyes. "Brought you a present. Well, two, actually."

Scott quirked an eyebrow and glanced around the park. "Out here?"

Laughing, Adam reached in his jacket pocket and carefully slid out something wrapped in grease-stained napkins. "Extra ketchup," he said, "from that cart you like near the college."

Scott's stomach growled in delight as he was handed the hotdog. "Oh my God. I think I love you." Scott looked at Adam and noticed how his boyfriend shied away at the lighthearted declaration. "Thank you," he added and leaned forward to plant a kiss on Adam's cheek. "You wanna share?"

Shaking his head, Adam smiled. "I ate already."

Scott tucked into the hotdog, and with the first bite of the ketchup- and mustard-smothered dog, he couldn't help but give a verbal yum *of appreciation. "Best present ever," he declared. He grinned through the mouthful of food and watched as Adam's smile widened. "What?"*

Adam leaned forward and raised his hand to Scott's face. His touch was gentle as he cupped Scott's cheek. Their eyes met and Scott was sure the rest of the world had melted away. It was just the two of them. Adam wiped his thumb over the corner of Scott's mouth. "A little mustard," he said. He pulled back his hand and then sucked his thumb clean.

God what this man did to him. Damn who was watching, he'd take Adam right now and here out in the open if he wanted.

"So, what's my other present?" Scott asked.

Adam reached into his jacket pocket and pulled out another napkin. This one was clean and neatly folded in half.

"More mustard?" Scott wondered and touched his mouth.

Shaking his head, Adam handed over the napkin. "For after your exams."

Scott unfolded the napkin and smiled. IOU some well-deserved fun. *"You know as soon as I've sat through that last exam I'm cashing this in."*

Adam nodded. "And I'll be waiting for you to do so. Whatever you want. I'm your man."

DARKNESS HAD LONG SINCE CLAIMED THE DAY AND THE moon hung heavy and golden in the sky. The light of it and the flashing of the small navigation system in the prow of the boat were the only things guiding Scott to the smudge on the horizon. Marsh Harbor wasn't a busy place on weeknights normally, but this was Friday and that meant bars and clubs with tourists. Sometimes Scott would enjoy a night in the town, scratch the itch, get drunk, enjoy the company of another guy. He always went home alone. Home to Sapphire Cay. This time, though, he would have a passenger.

He saw Adam standing dejectedly on the pier. He was staring out at the ocean but unlike Scott, who had a clear view of Adam under a light, it was unlikely Adam could see anything of him. This gave Scott the chance to look at the young man who had brightened his life for six short months. Not so young now, he must be around twenty-five, but he looked older. Scott guessed prison did that to a man.

The *Liberty* nudged the dock, and Adam stood up straight when Scott moved into the light thrown by the pier lamps. He smiled down at Scott—a hesitant smile.

"Climb down," Scott shouted up. He indicated the wooden ladder down from the side of the jetty. This wasn't where the *Liberty* usually docked. Wedding guests didn't want to traverse rickety steps, but Scott imagined Adam wouldn't have an issue. He didn't. Clambering down, Adam landed in the boat with a small jump that set the *Liberty* in a soft rocking motion. Adam immediately spread his stance to balance.

"I'll pay you back every penny," he immediately started in.

"I'm not lending you money," Scott said simply. He pushed them from the dock and the *Liberty* drifted away. The engines started easily and before Adam could get a word in, Scott was heading back slowly to open sea.

"What do you mean? You said you would loan me money so I could stay here until Monday morning. Where are we going?"

"I'm taking you to the Cay."

"I don't want to go," Adam said immediately. He knelt and peered over the side of the *Liberty*. For a moment Scott imagined Adam jumping in.

"Don't lean too far," Scott said seriously. "Sharks in this water."

Adam scrambled back and sat firmly in the middle of the boat. "You said you'd give me money," he said as soon as he was safe in the center.

"Likely I wouldn't get it back," Scott said.

Hurt flashed over Adam's face, followed quickly by resignation. Why was it the hurt didn't matter but the resignation poked a sharp stick in Scott's stomach? "I'd have repaid you every cent," Adam murmured. "But I understand why you don't think I would." Defeat colored Adam's words but Scott pushed away the instant feeling of sympathy. Then just as quickly blew it by talking.

"It's not the paying me back that I have a problem with," Scott said. Sure, Adam would have paid him back. Where he'd get the money to do so, that's what Scott had an issue with. "I know you would."

"No, actually you don't know a thing," Adam snapped. Jeez. Adam was apparently arguing for the sake of it.

"Look, I get you're pissed. The owner of Sapphire Cay, Dylan, offered you a room in the staff area for tonight, Saturday, and Sunday. I'll take you to Nassau on Monday."

All the fight left Adam in one big sigh of exasperation. "And so I'll owe them," he said. "I can't afford their prices," he added with a sigh.

"They won't charge you—we're allowed guests every so often."

"We're sharing a place—"

"God no. You have your own cabin."

"Oh. That's good," Adam finished weakly.

At least defeat was missing from his words. Instead, his clever mind, the one Scott knew Adam had, was likely thinking on this new turn of events. *How do I even know he's thinking?* Clearly, he recalled exactly how Adam looked when he was deep in thought. He wondered what other parts of Adam's personality he had hoarded away in his head. The memory of the noises he made when he was coming, the way he cooked omelets that tasted like heaven, the fact he never used his own shampoo and always stole Scott's.

I like to smell you on me all day, he had said when Scott asked why.

Scott had never been able to smell apple shampoo since without remembering Adam and his lies.

"Fifty minutes," Adam interrupted Scott's thoughts.

"Sorry?"

"The journey to Sapphire Cay, the sparkling jewel in the wide ocean, is fifty minutes." He used his fingers to imply quotes. "It says so on the website and blog."

Scott checked the navigation and made a small adjustment. Only a short while into this trip and he was finding out Adam had seen the blog. The one Scott wrote posts on. That was how Adam had found him. How? It wasn't like Scott put his full name on there.

"Simon told me where you were, and I looked it up. Your posts make me laugh. I feel like I know Dylan and Lucas and the wedding planner guy."

"Edward," Scott supplied with a smile.

"Yeah, he sounds like a cool guy. You write some good stuff on there."

"Thank you."

"One thing, though, why are you still here, what about your plants, the horticulture?" Adam asked.

Great. Did he lie or could he actually be honest with Adam?

"I wasn't ready to settle when I finished college," Scott said. "I went traveling, met up with Dylan, saw the world, and now I work at the Cay in season and travel where it's hot off-season." *Just like Dylan used to.* "I do some seasonal work in Singapore at the botanical gardens, and I have my research."

"Oh. Okay." Adam subsided into silence, and Scott concentrated on the steering of the *Liberty* and felt comforted that soon he'd have the buffer of Dylan, Lucas, and all the other staff between him and the man asking the questions.

"I'm sorry," Adam said in a low voice. "Sorry if what I did made you give up on what you wanted to do."

That pointed stick dug deeper and his stomach lurched. Suddenly angry that he even felt an ounce of compassion, he rounded on Adam.

"No, Adam. You never had that much power," he lied.

With that, he turned his back very deliberately on Adam and refused to give any indication that he would carry on with talking.

When the *Liberty* docked at the small jetty on the beach, Scott jumped off immediately, then tied her off. Without waiting, he began to walk up the beach toward the main hotel and heard Adam scramble off the boat and the sound of his rushed steps to catch up with Scott.

"I'm sorry," he said quickly. "I didn't mean to presume."

Scott stopped dead but didn't face Adam. "If you say sorry one more time I will push you in with the sharks," he snapped angrily.

"Okay. Sor—" He cut off the words.

"Guys," Dylan called from the door. Scott continued walking, and Adam followed quietly. Scott watched as

Dylan extended a hand and Adam shook it. "Welcome to Sapphire Cay," he said.

"Thank you for letting me stay. I thought Scott was just going to lend me some money but when he said you offered a space here…"

Dylan glanced at Scott with narrowed eyes. Scott shook his head imperceptibly. Knowing that it had been Scott who asked Dylan and Lucas for a place for Adam served no one at the moment.

"You're welcome. Sorry to hear about what happened. Are you hungry?"

"No," Adam said immediately.

"Yes," Scott said at the same time.

"Don't stand on ceremony. Scott knows where the kitchens are—help yourself."

"Where's Lucas?" Scott asked as Dylan turned to leave.

"Working," Dylan said. He looked back, then winked. "I'm just going to suggest a walk to the waterfall." He laughed and wandered off down the corridor toward the office. Scott turned left and led Adam to the kitchen. He rummaged in the large fridge, pulled out salad and meat, then bread from the larder. Placing the whole lot on the work surface, he turned to Adam to tell him to help himself. What he saw stopped him dead. Adam was turning in a slow three-sixty and he had a gleam of excitement in his eyes.

"Oh my God, this kitchen is gorgeous," he said. Then he ran his hands over the six-burner range, the stove controls, the stainless steel coffee machine, and finally turned to face Scott and leaned back on the nearest surface. "Dominiq is so lucky," he offered.

Scott opened his mouth to ask how he knew about Dominiq, then just as quickly recalled the blog entry he'd written about the exploding muffins.

"You were only helping," Adam said seriously. "You weren't to know that too much baking powder makes them go…" He indicated an explosion with his hands then smiled. "What I would give to work in a place like this."

"We have staff," Scott said immediately.

"I wasn't…I didn't…I mean, I wasn't hinting or anything." Adam turned from excited to awkward in an instant.

Jeez, what am I doing? Bringing him here to beat on him for three days or actually getting to some kind of resolution in my head.

"Help yourself," he said and indicated the fillings.

"I'm not hungry," Adam insisted.

Scott shook his head. "You're skinny as a rake. Eat."

Adam hesitated at first and appeared to be contemplating what he was doing. Finally, he crossed to the work surface and pulled together a ham and tomato sandwich without saying a word. He took his first bite and closed his eyes. An expression of pleasure crossed his face.

"Don't you eat?" Scott asked. "And you're so pale. Don't you ever see the sun?"

Adam lowered his sandwich to the plate. "Working in a kitchen and training doesn't get you as much food as you think. To be honest, you're so busy you forget, and no, there isn't much in the way of sun when you're inside all day." There was an edge to his voice. He was probably already tired of Scott's snappy bitchiness. God, Scott was pissed at himself as well.

"I apologize. It's not my place to comment," he said finally. Before Adam could reply, Scott scooped up his own plate. "Come on, I'll show you to your room."

They walked out of the main hotel and down the path to the staff area, to a row of small cabins in shadow of trees. They came to a halt in front of one of them with a sign saying 'Pupfish'. Scott smiled to himself. Lucas had threatened to return the cabins back to a simple naming of one, two, three… But Dylan had fought to keep the nod to the previous owners and their love of all things Bahamian.

"Your home sweet home," Scott said as he pushed open the door.

"Wow," Adam breathed. "This is gorgeous."

Scott glanced inside the open door. This was one of the basic staff cabins, little more than a bed, a closet, and a walk-in shower. But he supposed compared to the flea pit of a hotel Adam had been staying in this place was heaven on earth. "Make yourself at home. Wait here."

He jogged the small distance to his cabin, across and down four. Letting himself in, he moved to the closet and pulled out board shorts and a T-shirt. Grabbing a new pack of underwear, he went back to Adam.

Adam hadn't moved. He was standing at the threshold expectantly.

"I got you these for the morning." He eyed Adam critically. The guy had grown a few inches and lost the puppy softness that had rounded his face. The new look was edgy, yet so damn familiar. "Everything will be too big," Scott explained. "Maybe we have some other stuff I can find, maybe Edward left some tight stuff we can roll up the pant legs on."

"Okay." Adam clutched the clothes close. Scott fought the need to pull Adam into his arms and hug out some reassurance. Adam looked a little lost and wary.

"Stay in your cabin. No wandering around the place. We have guests here and they won't want to see you."

"Stay here. Got it."

"I'll come collect you in the morning."

"Okay."

Scott walked away to his own place and heard a small 'thank you' as he left.

Hell, at least it wasn't another attempt at sorry.

Chapter Six

ADAM TRIED TO STAY IN HIS ROOM. HE WOKE UP AT SIX AM and the sun called him. All he did was go outside his cabin. Then he moved a little farther away to look through the palm trees at the gorgeous pool. For a while he stood and watched the sun sparkling off the water. There was no sign of guests, but he wasn't going to chance a swim. Even if he had trunks. He glanced toward the sea, but Jaws lived in there, and while he may be stupid, he wasn't *that* stupid. Sighing, he turned to face the cabins. The blinds were drawn in Scott's cabin, and half of Adam, the half without self-preservation, wanted to knock on the door. The other part of him wanted to swim back to Marsh Harbor, killer shark in the ocean or not.

"Good morning," a voice said from behind him. Guiltily, Adam spun on his heel and came face to face with the man who could only be Dominiq. Tall, Bahamian, his wide smile was a welcome one.

"Hi, I'm sorry." Jeez, he couldn't keep saying that

word. It was like programmed into his instinctive response list or something.

"Dominiq," the other man said and held out a hand.

"Adam," Adam replied and shook his hand.

"Ah, Adam. Scott's friend."

"That would be me." He wasn't going to focus on the word friend.

"Coffee?"

"I can't, I'm not supposed to leave my cabin."

Dominiq grinned widely. "Let's break the rules."

He sauntered off, chuckling low under his breath, and Adam was mesmerized by the sound. Add in the lure of coffee and he was convinced that heaven was this island. He followed Dominiq and ended up back in the kitchen he had nearly drooled over last night.

Dominiq crossed to the coffee machine, and with deft movements he had fresh coffee perking. The instant fragrance hit was enough to have Adam crossing to the machine and grabbing a mug from the selection to the left of it. Gratefully, he filled his mug when Dominiq gave him the all clear, and then he sat on a stool at the counter. He was a little unsure about what to do next. Dominiq was busy whisking egg whites, then moved on to making biscuits from scratch.

"Can I help at all?" he finally asked. He was itching to get his hands on some of the wonderful gadgets in this place.

"Can you cook?"

"In the last few months of my final year in culinary school, and I work part time in a restaurant as well."

"Can you do scrambled eggs? Bacon?"

"Yes."

Dominiq regarded him carefully. "Wash your hands and grab one of my jackets from the storage area."

Adam did as he was told, and the two men fell into companionable silence as they worked, only speaking when Adam asked a question about where something was. He lost himself in the weights and measures and times, and for the first time in a few weeks he was back in his rhythm. His reason for coming here was to give Scott a chance to rail at him, ask him questions, maybe he'd be lucky enough to receive Scott's forgiveness. And maybe one more kiss. He was so lost in his thoughts he didn't immediately register Scott storming into the kitchen.

"What the fuck, Adam?" he snapped.

Adam startled and the bowl of dough he had at an angle to stir clattered flat on the surface.

"What?" he said quickly.

"I told you to stay in the room."

"I was helping Dominiq—"

"Lucas only let you stay because I promised I wouldn't let you wander around and steal anything."

It was true that words could hurt. But he deserved it. He knew that. He was used to it all.

"Scott, I asked him to help," Dominiq defended. Adam sent the big guy a smile of thanks.

"It's okay. Scott's right," Adam said quietly. "Thank you for letting me in here. I had fun." With as much dignity as he could muster, he pushed the bowl away from himself.

"No," Dominiq snapped. "My kitchen, my rules. Scott. Out."

"Dom—"

"Don't Dom me, this boy is working hard, and he's doing no harm."

"Lucas said—"

"If Lucas has an issue, send him to me."

Scott stood absolutely still. His expression narrowed, and he looked from Dom to Adam. "I'm on a supply run so I'm trusting you," Scott said finally. Then he spun on his heel and left the kitchen.

Now came the accusations from Dominiq.

"So, stealing, eh?" was all the big guy said. "You did time?"

"Three years," Adam admitted.

"How old were you when you went in?"

"Nineteen."

Dominiq nodded. "I was twenty," he said gently. "Did five for a bar fight that got out of hand. Get the biscuits done, service will be soon."

Evidently, Dominiq wasn't saying anything else, and he focused back on what he was doing. Adam did the same. Dominiq wasn't going to judge him based on facts alone, and that was kind of cool. Scott, however, was pissed at him, but he could live with that.

Scott had every right.

LEAVING THE SAFETY OF THE KITCHEN WAS HARD. DOMINIQ patted him on the back and thanked him for his help, and finally there was nothing he could do except return to the cabin and maybe sit outside. He'd have to sit in the shade a lot—he didn't have sunscreen, something else that was in his stolen backpack. They had some at reception, but it wasn't as if Adam had money to pay for it.

However much he had to stay in the shade, the idea of having somewhere to go where he could sit in peace for a little while was a welcome one. He'd almost lulled himself into the idea of sitting quietly and avoiding Scott.

Which was why it was so damn hard when he exited the kitchen and Scott was waiting for him, leaning against the wall with his arms crossed over his chest. He straightened when he saw Adam.

"We need to talk," he said.

A lump formed in Adam's throat as he braced himself for the reprimand. He knew Scott didn't want to hear it, but what could he say other than sorry? He was. Sorry he got his bag stolen. Sorry he had no one else to call for help. Sorry he couldn't follow one simple instruction. Sorry he was such a fuck-up.

"Not here," Scott said. "Let's walk."

Adam looked past Scott and down toward the beach. He was sure Scott was going to throw him to the fishes or maybe bury him neck deep in sand and wait for the tide to come in.

"Something wrong?" Scott looked annoyed at Adam's hesitation.

"No. Sor— I mean, everything's fine." He'd self-deprecate later. "Lead the way."

Scott narrowed his eyes. He looked baffled, but quickly dismissed Adam's behavior. Just another reason to think him a complete idiot, Adam chided himself.

"Did you have fun?" Scott asked as he headed for the path down to the beach. There was no harshness or mockery in his words. It appeared it was simply a question.

"Dominiq is great. Did you know he's had no formal training? He was taught by his mom and then by testing and tasting and making his own tweaks and recipes." He shut up. Scott probably already knew all that, and Adam was just coming across like some rambling moron.

"I didn't know," Scott said. "Though it doesn't surprise me. He's a law unto himself sometimes. I can't imagine him letting anyone tell him what to do."

"He likes to break the rules," Adam said.

Scott looked over his shoulder, slowing as he let Adam fall in beside him. They walked in silence as they descended the steps and made their way across the beach. Out to the small pier where the boat Scott had collected him in was moored. He followed Scott out onto the jetty. Scott sat down when he reached the end and dangled his legs over the edge. He seemed to be waiting for Adam to join him.

"I won't bite," Scott said and looked up at Adam and smiled.

"The sharks might." Adam peered over the edge suspiciously.

Scott smirked. "No sharks here," he said. "We have a natural barrier and the water is way too shallow."

"Oh."

Scott's smile slowly faded as he then added seriously, "I want to say I'm sorry for what I said in front of Dominiq."

"I didn't think we were saying sorry," Adam said dryly. He relaxed a little as he sat next to Scott and looked down at the clear water. Were there really no monsters beneath the surface?

Scott nodded. "But I am. I had no right to embarrass you like that."

"You had every right." These were Scott's friends, his family as he called them on the blog. Adam shouldn't be here disrupting their little slice of heaven.

"No, I didn't. I overreacted." He leaned forward and joined Adam in staring at the ocean.

"Thanks," Adam said.

"Whatever happened before, I'm willing to put it aside for the few days you're here," Scott said quietly.

Pain knifed through Adam. Scott saying he was putting how he felt to one side must mean he still hated Adam. He should have known that was how it would play out. He should be happy that Scott at least talked to him and not expect more from the man he wanted back in his life.

He swung his legs as he curled his fingers over the wooden edge of the pier. "It's really beautiful." He looked at Scott and smiled. The afternoon light cast a warm glow over Scott's tanned face. When Scott returned his smile, Adam decided if he died tomorrow he would die happy. He'd missed Scott so very much and to see him smile meant the world to him.

"You want a tour?" Scott said.

Adam grinned. "Sure."

"WELL?" SCOTT ASKED. HE RESTED HIS ELBOWS ON THE edge of the bar and waited. He and Adam had spent hours touring the east side of the island—the beach, the rock pool, the hotel, and the garden. Scott had talked and Adam had listened. He had talked about the island, about the plants he'd chosen while revamping the hotel—the ones that liked shade, the ones that adored the sunshine, and the various colors, scents, and meanings. "Do you like it?"

Adam sipped the cocktail and gave nothing away. He licked his lips and stuck out his tongue as he half choked. He looked at Scott through watering eyes. "What the hell is in that?" He released the bendy straw and sat back on his stool. He continued to lick at his lips.

Scott pulled the daiquiri toward him and tasted it. *Whoa.* Definitely too much rum. "You said you liked rum," Scott said with a laugh.

"Yeah, but wow. That's…" Adam laughed and waved his hands, refusing the drink when Scott offered it to him for a second try. "Please tell me you aren't in charge of the bar."

"Sometimes," Scott said.

"So, it's your fault for all the drunk uncles hitting on the bridesmaids," Adam stated.

Scott sighed and then took another drink. The taste might grow on him, eventually. "It's not that bad." Nobody had ever complained about his cocktail-mixing skills before. He held the straw and had another drink. The daiquiri tasted better with each try.

Adam grinned. "If you say so." His eyes brightened before he twisted on his stool and shyly looked away and beyond the pool. "What's that?" he asked and nodded toward the structure overlooking the ocean.

Scott raised his eyes and looked over the top of his

drink. He followed Adam's gaze and smiled around the straw. The time was a little after five and the early evening sun had dipped just below the line of trees, casting dark shadows over the gazebo. Walking around the bar, Scott curled his finger, indicating for Adam to follow him.

"Where are we going?" Adam slid off his stool.

"You'll see." Scott headed around the pool, across the patio area, and followed the path weaving between potted plants and large rocks down to where the gazebo stood. For a moment, he looked proudly at the metal and wooden structure. He and the others had done an amazing job rebuilding it in such a short time. He crouched down at the side of the gazebo and opened the plastic cover to the power switch before looking over his shoulder and waiting for Adam to join him. Flipping the switch, he watched Adam's face as two-dozen strings of fairy lights flickered to life. The white light illuminated the ground in a series of patterns and shadows as the lights faded off and on in a twinkling rhythm.

"Wow." Adam looked impressed. "Can I?" He pointed toward the gazebo.

Scott nodded.

Quickly, Adam took the steps up into the gazebo and wrapped his hand around one of the wooden struts. "It's very beautiful." He stepped inside and looked up at the ceiling. "It's like the night sky."

The lights had been left up after the last wedding. The gazebo had yet again been a beautiful backdrop for vows of forever and declarations of love. Old feelings came to the surface, and Scott wasn't sure what to do about them. Standing beneath the cocoon of lights, Adam looked like the young man from six years ago. He looked like the man Scott had loved and, in some ways, still did. "You blogged about rebuilding it. You and a guy named…" Adam pursed his lips as he tried to remember what he'd read. "Jamie," he finally said.

"Dylan helped," Scott said with a grin. Adam seemed in awe and the light gave him a youthful innocence. Had Adam ever been truly innocent? At what age had he reached the decision to go down the route he did? A path of lies and crime. Scott's smile faded as he realized how little he really knew about Adam. Scott's life was an open book, pages of which Adam had been able to read online through the Cay's blog. Was anything Adam had said the truth? Was he really in school? Was he really trying to turn his life around?

When they'd been together, within six months Scott had decided they were perfect for each other. He had really thought they had a future. Slowly, he turned away, looking back toward the hotel. The building held the security of familiarity. The hotel was solid and safe, and part of him wondered if he should run inside and lock the doors behind him. He closed his eyes as he heard Adam on the steps and sensed the man was now standing behind him. Memories of how it used to be reared inside him and he turned around. Scott looked at Adam and then back at the gazebo.

"Are you okay?" Adam asked. He looked wary, uncomfortable almost, as he met Scott's eyes. Had he seen the weight of memories and regret pressing down on Scott's shoulders?

Scott nodded and stared at the sparkling lights. *Damn you, Edward*. He'd never really appreciated the difference a string of fairy lights could make. Just a shift in mood and atmosphere, and then suddenly a simple wooden gazebo became the most romantic setting. Like a sky of blinking stars just for the wedding couple. He looked at Adam. Their stars. He knew he'd probably regret it in the morning, but his heart ached to recapture the feelings he'd lost what felt like a lifetime ago. He wanted to reignite that spark, no matter how brief, and remember the one time he truly felt for another person. He wanted to feel and touch and kiss.

Before either man had time to really acknowledge what it was they were doing, both stepped forward. Scott raised his hands, cupping Adam's face as he drew him in and kissed him. Adam's hands were in the back of his hair and his in Adam's. He stroked the nape of Adam's neck and moved upward until he found the thicker, longer hair behind Adam's ears. Electricity was in the air and Scott held onto Adam tight. Adam's stubble brushed his chin as the kiss deepened and turned to something openmouthed and hungry.

Damn, I missed this.

He held onto Adam's shoulders as he pushed him across the space and up against the side of the gazebo. Desperately, he kissed his old love. Even after all these years, the passion and flame was there. Adam was a hard man to forget and even harder to get over. Lost in the kiss, Scott enjoyed the taste and feel of the man against him. He roamed his hands over Adam's body, noting the curves and dips in all the right places. He stopped and held onto Adam's hips. *Too thin.* He leaned forward and felt Adam hard against him.

Opening his eyes, he reacted aggressively to the contact. They shouldn't be doing this. *He* shouldn't be doing this. Angrily, he pushed Adam hard in the chest, breaking the kiss and leaving Adam standing against the gazebo, wide-eyed and breathless.

They stared at each other and it was clear neither of them knew what to say. Scott stepped back and lowered his hands. He looked at Adam's face, his black eye, the plastic strips over the wound on his temple, and actual fear knotting his eyebrows together.

"I'm sorry," Scott said and backed away. This wasn't him. He didn't act like this. He wasn't some thug. He met Adam's eyes. The man looked as confused as hell. Scott ran a hand back through his hair. What had gotten into him? "You okay?" Scott reached out, intending to rest his hand comfortingly on Adam's shoulder and apologize some more. He barely touched him and Adam flinched.

Scott pulled back, surprised. "I won't hurt you."

Adam shook his head. "I should go," he said and pushed past Scott.

Not knowing what to say, Scott watched Adam as he made his way back up the slope and across the patio. What did he expect Adam to do? He was blowing hot and cold with Adam, and he had already hit him once.

"Fuck," he said. He was such an asshole.

Chapter Seven

ADAM SKIRTED THE CABINS AND MADE HIS WAY TO THE kitchens. He felt certain and safe there. The comforting presence of Dominiq and the fact that he didn't have to talk or feel awkward was half the battle. Luckily, Scott hadn't followed him when he left. What would he have done if Scott had decided he wanted to talk? What would Adam have said?

"Hey, little man," Dominiq said from the large walk-in fridge. "You doing good?" Adam smiled at the affectionate nickname. He was five nine and didn't consider himself really short, but then anyone was little compared to the big dude in the chef's whites.

"Did you want any help?"

Dominiq scanned the kitchen. "You can get on with the salads if you like. Dinner is in an hour, it's only staff tonight."

Adam washed up and grabbed a clean chef's coat. Intent on chopping greens, he was soon lost in thought. That kiss had been pure and sweet and hot, and then Scott had pushed him away. Of course he would push him away. Adam knew he wasn't the person Scott wanted or needed. He was okay with that. He hadn't expected rainbows and ponies when he found Scott—just closure.

Then he'd flinched. Great.

Scott had moved to touch him, but he had such an expression of intensity on his face that it freaked Adam out. Brought back memories of the encounters in prison that he'd managed to get away from only because he was small and fast. It also brought back the even more recent memory of Scott knocking him to the floor. He couldn't wait to get off the island.

He placed small cherry tomato halves in a bowl and tossed them in a vinaigrette that he concocted from oils and vinegar. Humming to himself, he wasn't even aware that Dominiq was next to him until the gruff voice was right in his ear asking him if he had moved the salt.

Adam ducked in shock, then stumbled back against the surface and slipped on his ass. His heart threatened to beat out of his chest, and he couldn't speak.

"Jeez, son, I'm sorry." Dominiq held out a hand to help him stand, but Adam wasn't quite ready to reach out and instead shrunk away. Dominiq crouched down, probably in an effort to appear smaller to Adam. Who the hell knew? All that he was aware of was the tumbled spread of cherry tomatoes and slick dressing and the fact Dominiq's shoe was buried deep in the squished red fruit. His heart refused to stop racing.

Stupid. Freaking stupid. What the hell is wrong with me?

"What happened?" Scott's voice broke through the

anxiety in Adam's head, and Adam added acute embarrassment to the panic attack. Dominiq moved so he was between Adam and Scott.

"Nothing," he said brusquely.

"Is Adam okay?" Scott asked. Adam couldn't figure out if Scott sounded pissed or sympathetic or just plain confused.

"Get the hell out of my kitchen, Scott," Dominiq stated simply.

"Dom—"

"Out."

Adam bowed his head in the absolute shame of what had just happened, and he didn't know if Scott had left or not. He was thankful Dominiq had his back. Dominiq stood and held out his hand again. This time Adam gripped hard to the offered support and allowed the big man to haul him to his feet. He'd smacked his knee on the way down and fuck, it hurt. Glancing down, all he could see was tomato and oil, but no blood.

"I can't say sorry enough," Dominiq repeated.

"You didn't do anything," Adam said tiredly. "I'm on edge after the bag snatch is all." He was lying but he hoped Dominiq didn't call him on it. "I'll clean this up and start again. Sorry."

Dominiq still had hold of his hand, and he pulled Adam in for a quick hug.

"You never have to say sorry to me, son," he said gently. Then he released his hold and they didn't talk again.

Preparation done and, with the staff filing in to eat, Adam

managed to fill the remaining time with enough busywork to not have to talk to Dominiq. Scott was one of the last to walk in, and he looked at Adam with a frown on his face. Adam refused to meet his gaze for a prolonged period and chose an empty seat at the opposite end of the table. No sense in putting himself in the firing line of a million questions.

So, he'd done time. So, he was a little fucked by it all. But, he'd gotten out and was making something of himself.

That was no one else's business but his own.

The only problem with sitting in this particular seat was that he was opposite Dylan and Lucas with all their flirty happy stuff. They were getting married, and the current discussion topic appeared to center around when would be a good time. On season, off season…the conversation at least gave Adam something to have as background noise while he lost himself to his own thoughts.

"WHAT'S THIS?" SCOTT HAD HIS HAND ON ADAM'S BACK, gently pressing against the pattern of old scars on his shoulder.

Adam lifted his head from the pillow and struggled to see where Scott was pointing. "Do you want the truth, or should I make something up so I sound interesting?"

Scott seemed to think and then shook his head. "Truth."

"When I was fourteen we had this dog. I'm not sure what the hell breed he was, something mixed with a horse.

He was massive. I tied him to the handlebars of my bicycle, and let's just say he took me for a walk."

Laughing, Scott traced his fingers over the grazed lines of the scar. Adam had been dragged for what felt like a mile, tangled up in his bike and the leash. "I never had a dog. No pets at all."

Adam rolled onto his side and met Scott's bright blue eyes. "We should get a dog." He pressed his lips into a line realizing how definite he'd sounded. A dog? What the hell was up with him? He'd be suggesting moving in together next. Fuck, he might as well just get on his knee and propose.

Scott didn't seem to care and leaned forward to kiss a line across Adam's shoulders and to his mouth. As Scott's mouth covered his, Adam wondered if Scott was the man to dream about doing all those things with. Closing his eyes, he wrapped his hand in the back of Scott's hair and pulled him close. Life and his parents had taught him happy ever afters didn't happen to people like him. But what if they could? He deepened the kiss, sliding his tongue against Scott's playfully before collecting Scott up in a hug and rolling them both over. He straddled Scott's thighs and gave teasing kisses. He linked his fingers in Scott's and pressed his lover's hands into the mattress. Slowly, he rocked his body and twisted his hips, pressing his ass down against Scott's hardening erection. With a grin, he slid backward and down between Scott's legs. He continued to hold onto Scott's hands and nudged his face against the soft flesh of Scott's balls before circling his mouth around Scott's dick. There was only one happy ending Adam was interested in right now, and that would probably be happening within the next ten minutes.

THE SCRAPE OF A CHAIR NEXT TO ADAM HAD HIM LOOKING to see Scott replace whoever had been sitting there before. Adam blinked at the man, then glanced to see that most people had left the kitchen while he hadn't been paying attention. Only a couple remained the other end of the long table, and the plates had all been cleared.

"You okay?" Scott asked. He sounded genuinely interested and concerned.

"I spilt the tomatoes," Adam replied quickly. The words were the first to come to his thoughts.

"Dominiq seemed concerned about you."

"Stop that," Adam snapped. He pushed his chair back and stood. "I'm tired." He left before Scott could call him on what the hell was going on. And when he added a quick jog back to his place, he was in with the door closed behind him before Scott could make any more stupid statements. Leaning back against the door, he felt a flush of embarrassment as he recalled what Scott probably saw.

How Adam was now with his easy-to-startle reflex was just one of the small things he had been left with after being inside. That and a scar on his left arm when he just wasn't quick enough to get out of the way in a fight in the kitchen where he worked. It hadn't even been his fight, but it had been him crouched on the floor, trapped next to a knife fight with blood spreading on the floor around him.

He banged his head back against the door and was

surprised when someone knocked back. Holding his breath he waited for a second or two.

"Adam?"

Dominiq's voice was soft and encouraging.

"Yes?" Adam answered quickly.

"You know where I am if you want to talk," Dominiq said. Then he added, "Night," and suddenly Adam was left in his small cabin with his own thoughts.

He'd thought he was over all the crap in his head. The first two years of culinary school had been hard when he jumped at every stupid little sound. But the third year, now halfway through, had been easier. He had barriers in place, he had breathing he could do, he had counseling.

So, what the hell happened in the kitchen?

He'd let his guard down. That was all it could be. Damn Scott and his sea-blue eyes and his soft words and the kiss and showing him exactly what he'd lost when he'd fucked up.

Maybe he wasn't cut out to be a chef. Maybe he would never have his dream of having his own kitchen. Maybe he was fucked. This was all too hard.

His cell vibrated on the bedside table and traveled a few inches with the noise before coming to rest on the very edge. Dylan had loaned him a charger. Dylan was a nice guy, so were Lucas and Dominiq. And Scott.

The cell vibrated again, and Adam moved before the damn thing danced off the surface and cracked onto the flooring. Knowing his run of luck, if it hit the wood, the piece of shit cell would shatter.

Two texts. Both from Bobby. Adam opened the first one.

'Got an easy one. Three thou, no questions, your type of car'

Adam hovered over the delete button. Three thousand would make up for the cost of this freaking side trip to find Scott. Enough to get the rent he owed paid up to date. Enough for the new knives he needed for the course finals —Japanese steel and six hundred dollars for just one.

How easy would it be to say yes. An 'easy one' was how Bobby described the cars that Adam had classified as belonging to owners literally too stupid to be trusted with their own vehicles. Not that he did anything like that in his head anymore. A car left with keys or given to a valet wasn't an easy mark. People worked hard for their cars. He was done with that shit. Done. Adam deliberately deleted the text and the second one opened automatically.

'Twenty-seventh, owner away, ordered grab, import, Nissan GT-R, 3k easy, C U usual place.'

Adam pressed the off button before he could read it again and placed the cell very deliberately on the surface of the cabinet.

He was done.

Chapter Eight

SCOTT FOUND DYLAN ON HIS HANDS AND KNEES UNDER the table in the office. He didn't bother asking why his friend was down there or even come up with a lewd suggestion about where Lucas might be. He was antsy and irritable, and tension held a tight hold on his neck and shoulders. Adam was getting under his skin again. Scott cared for him; he didn't think he'd ever really stopped, just fooled himself into thinking that the boy he'd fucked in college was out of his life.

Stupid. That was what he was. Physical work would take the edge off how he felt. He was sure of it. Still, after everything he'd done today on what was his day off, he was still feeling prickly and introspective.

"Dylan," he began.

Dylan sat up suddenly and smacked his head on the underside of the desk. He cursed loudly then peered over the top at Scott.

"What?" he asked.

"I fixed the hot tub, I've cleaned the pool filters, I've

done the supplies rotation for Dominiq, is there anything else I can do?"

Dylan looked up at him and frowned. "It's Sunday."

"Uh huh," Scott answered. Dylan sure liked to state the obvious.

"We don't have a huge guest list."

"Nope."

"It's your day off."

"I just need to keep busy."

Dylan raised his eyebrows but he didn't ask why. "What about the garden?"

"I can't do that." *It's too close to Adam's cabin and he could come out and talk to me and I'm not ready to get into that.*

"That's all I have," Dylan apologized. "We're doing well." Pride filled Dylan's words, and Scott couldn't help himself and smiled back. "Get lunch, go to the garden, work on your green stuff. I've got a printer to fix."

Scott left the office, dodging Lucas as he jogged toward him.

"Did you fix the printer for Dylan?" Lucas asked hopefully.

"No. He's working on it."

Both men heard Dylan's curse from the office. Lucas closed his eyes briefly. "You'd better warn everyone Dylan is at war with inanimate objects." Then he grinned at Scott, and, as soon as he was in the office with Dylan, he closed the door.

Scott made his way to the kitchen. Part of him hoped he didn't run into Adam, the other half hoped to God he did. The first half was lucky—there was no sign of Adam but Dominiq was at the sink with suds up to his elbows. Grabbing bread and ham, Scott made himself a sandwich and snagged a soda from the fridge. Idly, he joined Dominiq at the sink and leaned back against the work surface. He had a question, but Dominiq wasn't known for sharing secrets or gossiping. He had to think carefully and couch this question in indifference so that it didn't look like he was prying. Thing was, that was Adam on the floor with wide eyes and his hand pressed to his chest. He'd looked like he was slap bang in the middle of something pretty awful. In his head he had the perfect way to ask but what came out was actually something a little less fancy.

"What happened yesterday?" he blurted.

Dominiq flicked soap bubbles at him. Scott was shocked as the great big glob of detergent slid down his nose and dropped on his top.

"Go ask Adam," Dominiq said firmly.

"He won't talk to me."

"You talk with him?"

"I did."

"With him or at him."

Scott's mouth fell open. What did Dominiq mean 'at him'? Scott hadn't talked 'at' Adam. He'd asked questions and almost felt like he was back in the shitty apartment on the Ithaca campus.

"I don't know… I talked with him."

"You listen?"

Scott frowned in thought. He recalled what they talked about before the "tomato incident", as he labeled it in his head. He remembered the absolute romance of standing under the gazebo with the lights above them. Had they really talked about anything in particular? Or did Adam just listen? Scott knew he'd ruined it when he'd blown hot and cold with the kiss. He should never have kissed Adam when he had no inclination to carry the kiss into anything further. Although kissing Adam had been everything he remembered and more. Where before he'd kissed a boy, now he was kissing a man, with years since their last embrace that Scott knew nothing about. Including prison. The tomato incident was probably entirely Scott's fault.

"Maybe not," Scott admitted finally. Suddenly he wasn't hungry and he slid the sandwich into the trash before putting the plate in the dishwasher. "He won't answer my questions. He's evasive."

Dominiq shrugged. "Maybe you're not asking the right questions then."

With Dominiq's words ringing in his ears, Scott made his way to the garden area. Lovingly cultivated by his own hand, the large area curved away from the hotel and around the back of the cabins. Buttonwood, Seven-year Apple, Sea Hibiscus, and a profusion of gloriously colored Fire Bush formed a canvas that Scott could stare at all day. This was his peace. He turned a full three-sixty and checked each area. The Hibiscus needed thinning out if they were to survive against the sturdy Apple. He closed his eyes and stretched his arms high to unkink his neck. When he opened his eyes, he came face to face with Adam, who had clearly watched him do the whole turning-in-circles-stretching thing.

"Hey," Adam said quietly. "Dominiq came to tell me you wanted to see me? Said you had some questions for me?"

Scott signed inwardly. He'd been set up by the chef with the meddling actions and the big heart. Gesturing to a seat half-hidden by leaves, all he said was "Sit. It's peaceful here."

ADAM DID AS HE WAS TOLD. SITTING, HE WATCHED SCOTT gently nudge plants to one side as he sought out weeds from among the brightly colored flowers and lush greenery. Adam had no idea how Scott could tell what was weed and what was plant, some of the unearthed weeds looked as beautiful as anything else in the garden. The silence between them wasn't uncomfortable as such, but Adam had the urge to break it. Scott, after all, had called him here.

"What did you want to know?" he finally asked. He leaned forward to rest his elbows on his knees and looked thoughtfully at the back of Scott's head. He smiled at the memory of lazy Sunday mornings in each other's arms and the feel of Scott's hair between his fingers.

Scott didn't say anything at first as he sat back on his heels and rested his hands on his hips. He didn't turn around.

What more did Scott want from him? He didn't know how else to apologize, how to make things okay between them again. Though he knew they'd never have what they'd lost, he wanted them to be able to look back and remember the good things. He wanted forgiveness, closure, and just the smallest piece of evidence Scott believed him. Because what the hell was the point otherwise? How was he supposed to be a better man if neither he nor Scott could believe it?

"Do you want me to go?" Maybe Dominiq had been wrong. Maybe Scott didn't want to talk.

"No," Scott said and looked back over his shoulder. His eyes were narrowed as he met Adam's. "I don't want you to go."

There was a look in Scott's eyes Adam couldn't quite figure out. He really didn't want to fight anymore. In fact, he had very little fight in him these days. "Okay," he said carefully. He looked at the pile of discarded weeds. He knew how it felt to be thrown to one side. Scott got to his feet. Adam looked up. *So tall. So handsome and strong.* He also knew how it felt to be loved and wanted. God, he'd had so much to live up to back then. He'd wanted to give Scott the life he deserved. Not the one you led when earning minimum wage flipping burgers in some greasy diner.

Scott came to sit beside him, pushing away the growth of vines as he slid his six-foot frame into the space next to Adam. "If I ask you some questions, will you be honest with me?"

Adam swallowed the uncomfortable lump in his throat. It scared him to think exactly what Scott wanted to know. "I won't lie to you," he said. "I promise you that." Whether he could tell Scott everything, he didn't know, but what he did tell him would be the truth.

Scott seemed to accept his answer and turned his body as he faced him. "What happened yesterday?"

Adam narrowed his eyes and shrugged. "When?" More than he cared to remember had happened yesterday. The worst had seemed to be on permanent replay last night leading to little sleep and a walk along the beach at three in the morning.

"With Dominiq. You looked—" Scott took a breath and met his eyes. "Scared."

"I told you. I knocked over the tomatoes."

"And what? Did you think Dominiq would go all Hulk on you?"

Adam looked away across the garden. It was easier to say nothing than try to explain what was going on inside his jumbled head.

"Why won't you talk to me?"

Adam snorted a laugh. He'd tried talking for the last few days. He was done with talking. Tired and stuck in a place he didn't know, he just wanted to get to the embassy and then home. "Do you really want that?" he asked.

"Of course I do. We may have gotten off to a crappy start, but I'm concerned about you. I care—" Scott stopped and leaned back in his seat. "I care about you."

Adam tightened the muscles of his jaw as he weighed his options. Never appear weak. He'd learned that the hard way. Unconsciously, he rubbed at the inside of his left arm. He couldn't look at Scott as he finally said, "He caught me by surprise."

Scott didn't say anything and Adam was kind of relieved Scott was letting him talk in his own time.

"You know what the hardest thing about prison was for me?" Adam asked. He felt out the scar and rubbed his finger across the raised skin. "Knowing I was alone." Lowering his head, he stared at the ground. "No one to have my back on the inside and no one who gave a shit outside." He sensed Scott bristle behind him. "I know that was my own fault. I get that." He didn't blame Scott.

"Did something happen?" Scott's words were draped in unease.

Adam frowned and shook his head. "Not like that. But you know me, I feel threatened and I run my mouth off. Was only a matter of time before it caught up with me." Finally, he found the courage to turn around. Scott looked concerned and somehow that meant more than he could ever explain. "For three years, I was constantly watching my back. It's a hard habit to break." He pursed his lips. "My bag was stolen, you hit me—which I know I deserved." Scott shook his head in denial, but Adam forged ahead. He had to say what he expected Scott wanted to hear—that Adam took responsibility. "My mind has been preoccupied since getting here. Dominiq caught me in a moment where my guard was down and my focus elsewhere."

Scott smiled. "What were you thinking about?"

Adam shrugged. "I don't know. You, me, life."

"Sounds deep." The rich tone of Scott's voice soothed Adam.

"Too deep," Adam said with a laugh.

"I like deep."

Adam wasn't so sure. All it did was make his head and his heart hurt. So much so, he was ready to jump in the ocean and take his chances with the sharks. Anything to put some distance between him and Scott.

Scott shifted in his seat and looked firmly into Adam's eyes. He clearly had more questions. "Did you ever love me?"

Love. Had it been love? He chose his words carefully. "Maybe. You made me happy, and I'd have done anything for you." He closed his eyes. "I did do things for you. Stupid things that I wish I could take back."

"So what happened to you is my fault?" There was an edge of hurt in Scott's incredulous voice.

Shaking his head, Adam said, "That's not what I meant." He sighed. "*I* didn't feel good enough. *I* wanted to treat you like you deserved. *I* decided to steal those cars. It was easy money, and I could buy all the friends and love I wanted."

"You're an idiot," Scott said with a sigh.

Adam couldn't help but smile. "I know," he agreed. "And I paid the price." He tilted his head slightly as he gazed into Scott's eyes. *So very beautiful.* "And I don't mean three years." He'd lost Scott and it had hurt like hell. No visits, no letters. It was as if a whole chapter of his life had been torn out, and without it, he'd felt incomplete.

"You lied to me," Scott said grimly.

"I know."

"For months."

"I know," Adam said again.

"I loved you. I wanted us to be together. To travel. To build a future."

Adam snapped, "I know, okay? I said I was sorry. I don't know what else I can say or do—" He was shut up by Scott's hands on his face and Scott's mouth covering his. Wary at first, he let Scott kiss him. Scott's touch was rough, almost angry, but gradually, the heated temper of the kiss melted away, leaving only softness and a warm passion. Closing his eyes, Adam lowered his guard and kissed Scott back. He brought his hand up to twist in the back of Scott's dark hair and gently massaged the nape of Scott's neck. How he'd missed Scott—the man's taste and touch and everything in between. Given time, he would have said the words six years ago. He would have said *I love you*.

They parted momentarily. "I've missed you so much," Adam half whispered. "I knew you would hate me, and that tore me apart."

"I didn't hate you," Scott said carefully. Then he sighed, he'd asked Adam to be honest and he had apparently decided it was only fair he was honest in return. "Maybe I did."

Beneath the warmth of the sun, they kissed and touched and absorbed everything of each other. The way Scott kissed him, Adam knew his old lover felt exactly how he did. The spark of attraction and the surge of memories had desire shooting to the head of his dick. He remembered how it felt to have Scott fill him, to have Scott fuck him. Such good memories.

Scott's kisses softened and grew further apart, until eventually, he pulled back again. He looked at Adam with a hesitant desperation. It was clear he wanted Adam just as much as Adam wanted him, yet there was still doubt in his eyes. Scott had yet to decide if he could truly trust Adam and his good intentions.

"I can't go through that for a second time," Scott said. "Please don't lie to me."

Adam shook his head. "I promise."

"You're really done with all that?"

Nodding, Adam wrapped his hand around Scott's and

squeezed it tightly. "I'm finished. If you give me a second chance I won't let you down." He meant it. He really did. Hell, he'd delete Bobby's number and never speak to the man again. He'd move away wherever Scott wanted.

Scott chewed on his lip, and after a moment got to his feet, pulling Adam with him. "You mess me about and not even Dominiq will stop my tearing you a new one."

"Okay."

"No more lies or sneaking around."

Adam nodded.

"And no more of this *I'm not good enough for you* crap."

"I can do that."

Scott rested his hands on his hips and worried his lower lip between his teeth. His face relaxed, and Adam could imagine the little voice inside his head saying, *'What the hell?'* Scott stepped forward and wrapped his hands around Adam's waist, lifting him slightly off the ground as he pulled him into a tight hug and openmouthed kiss.

Adam circled Scott's neck, linked his hands and held on tight. He curled his fingers in the material of Scott's T-shirt and lost himself in the heat of the kiss. The pressure of Scott's body against his drove him crazy. He could feel the hard press of Scott's erection against his thigh as his own dick firmed from the urge to have his ex-lover deep inside him, making love as they used to. He wanted the touches, the thrusts, the hot, sweaty passion they used to have. God he'd missed this man so fucking much.

"My cabin?" Scott asked breathlessly. Adam could only nod wordlessly. Scott guided Adam across the garden and toward the staff area.

Shit. This is really happening. How is this happening?
Adam stiffened and caught Scott's face, cupping his jaw as he looked deep into the man's eyes. He really did want this and he nodded to let Scott know. Scott took Adam's hand in his and pulled him by the arm. This time, Adam decided, he'd do things right.

Chapter Nine

ADAM WAS DAZED. AS SCOTT TUGGED HIM ALONG THE path, he couldn't quite believe what was happening. Somehow Scott had listened to Adam's apologies and believed every word Adam said. The heady feeling of trust was something that had eluded him for so long.

He was the ex-con sponsored into a work and education program in culinary arts. He'd spent the first year there proving himself because even though he was consistently better than his peers, he still had the label attached to his name.

Adam? You mean the guy who was in prison. He doesn't look like a criminal? Heard there were guns involved. He's probably an ex–gang member. Does he have tattoos? Does anyone know what he actually did? Did he kill someone? We should keep an eye on him.

Adam had heard it all. Seemed people felt that being in prison made him deaf to their assessment of his character. Finally, he made friends; after nearly three years of just keeping his head down, his peers judged him as the nice guy who was the most creative student in the class. He'd gotten to the point where people wanted to know him for being Adam. But he hadn't found total trust, and he'd never met the right man.

He'd never needed just any man, and that was the problem.

He'd wanted Scott.

And now they were here.

Scott pushed open the door to his cabin and dragged Adam through before pushing the flimsy door shut then shoving Adam up against it. The press of wood against his back and the dominant push had Adam near whimpering. He wanted this so bad. They kissed like they had never parted. Adam reveled in the taste and the touch and buried his fingers in Scott's hair to hold on tight. Scott pulled back, his face taut with need.

"Strip," Scott ordered. Adam was only too happy to comply. He removed his jeans, then pulled off his shirt. He automatically circled his heavy dick, which was way past ready and close to losing it straight away. "Don't touch yourself," Scott added. Adam immediately loosened his grip and reluctantly left his cock without touch.

"Scott…" Adam breathed. Was Scott punishing him somehow for what had happened? Would he be forced to stand here and hope that Scott would touch him? He deserved it. He needed—

"Stop it," Scott ordered.

"Wha'?"

"I can see it in your eyes," Scott said gently. He closed the small gap until his fully clothed body was close to

Adam. "Do you remember when we made love in my shitty apartment at college?"

Adam nodded. He thought maybe it was a trick question, but God yes, he remembered. Scott dragging it out, taking him to the edge then easing him back until finally Adam couldn't stop the orgasm that ripped through him.

Scott cupped Adam's face and his blue eyes held a compassion and need that scared Adam.

"You remember how you would lie in front of me," Scott said. "Touch yourself, and I would stand there and watch." Scott kissed Adam. "I had never seen anything so beautiful."

"I remember," Adam said softly. That was his favorite part, showing Scott what he was doing, arching off the bed, tensing his muscles as he reached around. And he'd watch back, watch his lover, watch Scott hold himself and move his hands the full length of his wide cock, turned on by Adam's display.

"You loved it when I told you what to do. When I crossed over and squeezed lube onto my fingers and I pressed them inside you, next to you, and you would make these sexy noises of need. Do you remember?"

"Scott," Adam moaned. He wanted that. Now. This wasn't punishment, this was the game they played and fuck, it was hot. "Please."

"I'm telling you to get on the bed, and I want you to play with yourself, and I want to watch and lick you and suck you and twist and pull your nipples until you're nearly coming just from that."

"Please."

Scott released the gentle cradling of Adam's face then took a step back. "On the bed, Adam," he demanded.

Adam scrambled to do what he was told and turned just in time to see the lube tossed alongside condoms.

"Open yourself for me."

Adam arranged himself with pillows propping his head and grabbed the lube. Slicking his fingers, he wasted no time. A gentle touch to his heated cock, a slide over his balls, then he pressed against his hole. So long. He'd done nothing, not even used a dildo. Not since that night when everything had gone to hell. The first finger inside him was nothing, but as he pushed deeper and added a second, he welcomed the burn. The whole time he stared at Scott, who slowly removed his clothes, then stood with his hand circling his thick cock. Adam whimpered.

"I want to suck you," he said as he pressed a third finger inside himself. He had to have a taste of Scott.

Scott looked to be debating the request and Adam added a breathy *please*. Finally, Scott kneeled on the bed next to Adam, and without ceremony he pushed himself past Adam's lips.

"Make it good," Scott said firmly. The first taste of Scott caused an explosion of memories and need, and tears pricked Adam's eyes. Ruthlessly, he forced the memories aside. Scott appeared happy to stay absolutely still, and Adam used his mouth as best he could. Scott shifted slightly and Adam tensed, concerned that Scott was pulling away. He had every argument under the sun in his head to defend a need to have his lips and tongue on Scott. Instead, Scott slicked his fingers and slowly ran them the length of Adam in a repeat of what Adam had done. He spent longer caressing Adam's sac, rolling his balls gently, then tugging and causing Adam to arch at the sharp pain.

Scott massaged the skin, then moved back to twist his little finger with Adam's. "Only three?" he whispered. His voice was a low growl. "Used to be you could use four, then me..." He didn't push inside alongside Adam at first. He began to move his cock in Adam's mouth, and when Adam was concentrating on his breathing and the absolute ecstasy of having Scott in him, it was the right time for Scott to add a finger of his own. The burn was enough to have Adam whimpering, but Scott didn't stop. Scott clearly still knew exactly what Adam wanted, and Adam wanted the burn, the reminder of what Scott could give him and what he could give Scott. He widened his legs and tilted his pelvis, and the fingers slid deeper. Scott unerringly located his sweet spot, and Adam saw stars.

"Fuck," Scott groaned. "I missed this, missed you..." He removed his finger and traced it back up Adam's stomach and chest, then concentrated on pinching Adam's nipple. The loss of the finger in his ass had Adam whining a protest around a mouthful of cock and he replaced the space with his little finger and forced it inside to his knuckles. He was so close, his ass clenching around the fingers and hardwired to his nipples. Scott knew. He always knew. He pulled himself free of Adam's mouth, and in seconds he had a condom rolled on his length and he pressed the blunt head against Adam's stretched hole and fingers. Adam pulled his fingers out, and immediately Scott was inside, his thick cock replacing them. Adam rolled his hips and tilted back a little more, and he stared up into Scott's sapphire eyes.

Words of love were on his tongue, but would Scott stop if he said them? Scott went deeper, and the rhythm he set was fast and hard. The initial pain of intrusion had become something else. Pleasure coursed through his body as Scott pegged his prostate over and over.

"Keep your eyes on me, Adam," Scott said. His voice sounded broken and he was breathless—his skin sheened with the exertion. Adam didn't break his focus even as his balls drew up and orgasm twisted inside his body. He wanted to see Scott coming inside him, but when he couldn't hold back anymore, he came so hard he nearly closed his eyes. Scott stilled, then cursed as he filled the condom before collapsing on top of Adam. The weight of him was perfect and Adam gripped Scott hard to stop him from moving.

"I love you," he said. He didn't know what he was expecting, but when Scott lifted his head he had a wide grin splitting his face.

"I love you too," Scott said and still smiled. "Hell, I missed you so much."

"I missed you too," Adam said. He screwed his eyes shut when those damn tears threatened to force their way past his lids and had to stop himself from adding an *I'm sorry* on the end of the sentence. Back at the apartment they used to fall asleep in this position, but this time Scott reached between and dealt with the condom. Then he sighed deeply and nestled his face back in the juncture of Adam's shoulder and neck.

Sleep came easily and Adam had nothing but good dreams.

SCOTT WOKE SLOWLY AND REALIZED AT SOME POINT IN THE evening they had moved so he was spooning Adam from behind. He pressed a kiss against his lover's shoulder and smiled. How could he ever imagine another day without Adam? The boy had become a man, and Scott loved the man he'd become as much as he had once loved the boy. His bladder demanded he move, and reluctantly, he slid his arm out from where it was trapped under Adam. His lover snuffled in his sleep and turned on his front. Scott admired Adam's back from the shoulders down to the dip just above his perfect ass. For a moment, he let himself believe it was younger-Adam lying on the bed beside him, and he remembered back to when things had been new and untainted.

Rolling off the mattress, he got to his feet. He used the bathroom and caught sight of himself in the mirror. He peered closer and wondered what Adam saw when he looked at Scott. They had so much to talk through, not least of all getting Adam to see that Scott had reached a happy balance in his life and that he wanted Adam to get to that point. Dominiq always moaned on about being the only one in the kitchen and how he had no help, maybe Scott could call in a favor and get Dylan to hire Adam for food and lodging or something like that.

Then maybe he and Adam could travel? Set up a restaurant somewhere like Adam wanted? Maybe Scott could actually use his degree in horticulture from Cornell and get a job near Adam's work? Anything really so that Adam was still in Scott's life. Permanently.

He drank some water and crossed back to the bed. A cell phone was on the floor next to Adam's discarded jeans, and Scott picked it up to place it on the bedside table. Knowing him he'd stand on Adam's only contact with the outside world. He didn't mean to look at the message that was timed as being received a few minutes ago. He didn't. But the short words on the screen were there in green.

'Call me. EASY money, GT-R, 3k.'

Scott shut the screen down and sat on the edge of the bed. This was the test. He could react in two ways. He could have absolute trust in Adam and see for himself that Adam hadn't answered the text. Or he could think Adam was fucking him over again. They'd talked of trust. Scott was trying his very hardest to trust Adam. But the small prick of doubt was there. For a while Scott sat there and contemplated what the hell he was doing.

Adam shifted in the bed and blearily looked at Scott. It appeared he didn't immediately realize where he was, then just as suddenly he grinned when he saw Scott. He looked exhausted but happy, and there was nothing wary in his expression. Scott liked that.

"Hey," Adam said with a sudden frown. "You okay?"

Chapter Ten

ADAM REGRETTED ASKING SCOTT THE QUESTION. SCOTT looked thoughtful and a frown creased his forehead. Was there something wrong? Had he done something? Or did Scott regret sleeping with him already?

"I'm fine," Scott said. He smiled as if he knew what had been running through Adam's head. "I just needed to pee." Adam could have sworn there was something hesitant in the way Scott looked at him, but then just as quickly it was gone and Scott returned to bed.

Adam welcomed him with an outstretched arm, relieved when Scott slid into the space and settled his head against his chest. He'd missed having someone to hold, someone to love. Love? Though he had never admitted it before, he could see now that he'd had love in his heart for Scott. He'd just been too stupid, too young and unsure to see what had been right in front of him. What they'd had fit just right and fuck if it still didn't. Scott knew how to touch him, how to have him touch himself. And to have that now, after everything, Adam knew he was the luckiest man alive. He wouldn't risk losing that, not again. He'd be the biggest idiot going if he did anything to break the trust Scott was placing in him right here, right now.

Scott dragged his fingers in circles across Adam's chest and nestled closer. With a sigh, he asked, "What time do you need to be at the embassy?"

Closing his eyes, Adam threaded his fingers in the back of Scott's hair. This morning he could hardly wait to get off Sapphire Cay, but now the prospect of having to leave made his heart ache in his chest.

"They open at nine," he said and opened his eyes. He stared up at the ceiling and wondered what Scott would want him to do. Originally, this was supposed to be as short a stay as possible, get a loan from the embassy, and find somewhere to stay in Nassau until his new documents came through. But they'd swapped *I love yous* and surely that changed everything.

He laid a kiss on Scott's forehead and dared to say, "Once I've applied for my passport, do you think Lucas and Dylan would be cool with me coming here to be with you for a couple of weeks? If they said it was okay, would you want me to stay?"

Scott stopped moving his hand and gently curled his fingers against Adam's chest. *Was Scott having second thoughts already?* Adam's fears were allayed as Scott simply said, "Okay."

"Thank you." That would give him two weeks to prove to Scott just how serious he was about making things right. He would be honest and do whatever Scott needed him to do. This was perfect.

Scott breathed in deeply and rolled away from Adam. "Too warm," he said sleepily and turned his back to Adam.

Rolling onto his side, Adam kept the sheet between them and gently rested his arm over Scott's waist. He smiled to himself and closed his eyes as Scott's fingers slid between his in a loose hold. Perfect.

WHEN ADAM WOKE, HE WAS SURPRISED TO FIND HIMSELF alone. With a smile on his face, he stretched out across the bed. He couldn't remember the last time he'd had a full night's sleep and it felt amazing to wake up and feel like he'd actually slept. He lay in bed and listened. Apart from the sound of his own breathing, there was only silence and Adam realized Scott must have gone out already, leaving him in bed.

Throwing back the covers, Adam rolled his legs over the side of the bed and sat for a moment. He stared at the thinly draped window and the brilliant sunshine outside. He had no idea what time it was but figured Scott would return for him when it was time to leave. Standing, he stretched his arms above his head. He'd missed this, the low ache of his muscles and the feeling of having had Scott inside him. The ache of the stretch and burn of him buried balls-deep, wide and filling Adam.

Shit. Adam groaned as the memory sprang to his dick and he was hard. He needed a shower. *A cold shower.* Crossing the room, he grabbed his clothes and what he assumed was a clean towel neatly folded on the dresser, and then headed for the bathroom and the shower.

Stepping under the spray, Adam immersed his face

beneath the water and slowly rubbed at his skin, tentatively soothing a line over his swollen brow and eye. He then pushed the water back through his hair and moved his head from side to side, enjoying the relaxing warmth of the water. Scott's shampoo sat on the shelf in the shower, and Adam was keen to remind himself of the scent of his lover. Opening the bottle, he inhaled the sweet scent. Where it had used to be apples, the scent was now more citrus and as he breathed in the smell, he realized it wasn't quite right. Scott also smelled of the ocean and something that was uniquely Sapphire Cay, all exotic plants and sunshine. He imagined Scott out there now, hefting trees and sailing across the ocean. With a smile, he massaged some of the shampoo into his scalp. The orange- and lemon-scented suds rolled over his body, slick and soapy as he roamed his hands downward. His erection was still there, hard and heavy as he circled his dick and gave it short tugs.

What am I doing? Scott could come back. What the fuck would he think to catch Adam smothered in his shampoo and jerking himself off in his shower? *He'd probably join me.* The thought of Scott's beautiful, firm, tanned body slicked and rubbing against him beneath the water had Adam pulling more firmly at his length. Damn, he was so fucking horny, caught up in the romanticism of Sapphire Cay and the imagined touch of his lover. "Fuck," he hissed and threw back his head. Spreading his legs, he reached behind him with his other hand, desperately trying to elicit the feeling of having Scott in him. Not that it mattered, just the thought had him moving roughly over his dick, bringing himself off with a stilted moan as he rested his hand against the tiled wall for support.

Breathless, Adam leaned his head back. The powerful spray of the shower hit his balls, making his cock twitch. Carefully, he reached down and massaged the sensitive area, closing his eyes as he ran his fingertips the length of his flaccid, spent cock. He needed to find Scott. He needed to show Scott exactly what he was doing to him. The thought of two weeks together full of sex and *I love yous* made Adam's heart skip contently in his chest. This would be good for him and for them. He wanted his old life back. Not the one of lying and cheating but the happy moments in Scott's arms and having amazing sex and whispers of a possible future together. He wanted that more than ever and he was determined nothing would ruin it. Not this time.

"WHAT IS WRONG WITH YOU?" LUCAS ASKED WITH A HUFF. "You dropped that on my head."

Scott looked down at the old garland that draped Lucas. He was so distracted this morning and he quickly apologized. "Sorry. Was thinking."

"It's Adam, right?" Lucas guessed as he pulled the garland of flowers from around his neck.

"Kind of," Scott said. He jumped down from the stepladder, taking the dry and browning decoration from Lucas and spiraling it into a ball on one of the tables in the dining room. "Why don't you just get plastic ones?" He eyed the string of dead flowers.

From nowhere, Lucas smacked Scott upside the head.

"Hey," Scott complained and glared at Lucas. "What the hell was that for?"

Lucas picked up one of the wilted flowers. "Plastic? Seriously? Call yourself a horta…horto—" Lucas rested his hands on his hips. "Call yourself a plant person?"

Scott grinned. "Horticulturist," he said.

"Thanks." Lucas tossed the flower back on the piled-up old garland. "You know Dylan likes them fresh. They smell great, and like Edward says, it's all about the little details. Guests notice and appreciate it." With a sigh, Lucas pulled out one of the dining chairs and took a seat. "Well, go on then."

"What?"

"Look, I might not be all Zen like Dylan or look wise and knowing like Dominiq, but you can talk to me." Lucas nodded toward the seat opposite, indicating for Scott to take it.

It wasn't that Lucas was hard to talk to. It was more the fact he was very logical and straight down the line, more black and white than shades of gray. Scott looked at the chair. Maybe that's what he needed. An answer that was more direct than *follow your heart and chase down what you want*.

"Okay," Scott said and sat. He looked at Lucas. What should he even say? "I slept with him."

Lucas quirked an eyebrow. That was clearly not what he had been expecting to hear. Lucas scratched behind his ear and rested his head in his hand. "Was it good?"

Scott's turn to be surprised. "Erm, yeah, it was. It was really good." The sex was as it used to be—hot, amazing, Adam doing everything Scott needed, wanted, and more.

He looked at Lucas, he obviously thought this was going to be some normal conversation, maybe throw in a few digs about Adam and an *I told you so*.

"And the reason I was wearing the old garland is…?" Lucas was looking for more reasons for Scott's inattention than just amazing sex. Apparently, just that on its own wasn't a good enough reason for Scott to be distracted from his morning tasks.

"I'm scared he'll disappoint me." There he'd said it. He was scared. He wanted to believe Adam and he had. The emotions that had radiated off his lover—the need, the love, the honesty.

Lucas shrugged. "Do you have any reason to think he will?"

There it was. Should he tell Lucas about the message on Adam's phone? That was the crucial detail. The one that would have Lucas telling him to run for the hills.

"I found a text."

"You were in his phone?"

"Not on purpose. It was just there." It really had been.

Lucas snorted a laugh and sat back. "You slipped and fell on it and all his messages popped up."

"It's not funny."

"I think it is," Lucas said. "If you don't trust him then that's a serious problem. It won't matter how many times he tells you he's changed. Do you think he's a good person now? If you can't believe that then the two of you won't stand a chance."

Logical Lucas. Damn. "You didn't ask what the message said?"

Lucas shook his head. "And if you told me? What do

you want me to say?" Lucas leaned forward, his amber eyes holding a smile as he said, "I'm not going to tell you he's lying to you, and I'm not going to tell you he isn't. I think that's something you need to decide for yourself. You need to ask him."

"He'll know I looked at his phone." How would that look? One minute he was saying *I love you* and *I trust you* to Adam and the next he was invading his privacy and looking for something to catch Adam out with.

"Well, that's down to you. You either ignore it and have this idea eating away at you. You end things with him without explanation. Or you talk to him and admit what you did, finding out the truth one way or the other."

Seriously, these were the only options Lucas had? "Is there an option where I don't tell him, find out the truth anyway, and therefore get to have amazing sex with him until I do?"

Lucas looked at him blankly.

I guess not.

"Just talk to him, you big idiot," Lucas said and got to his feet. "Take him to the embassy, then have a nice lunch, a walk along the beach, find somewhere quiet, and then 'fess up."

Scott sat, openmouthed, and could only watch as Lucas walked away from him. What the hell had just happened? Rubbing at his brow, Scott stood and pushed his chair back under the table. He ducked down and looked out the window and toward the path leading to the staff accommodation. He hated that Lucas was right. He'd asked Adam to be honest, and he guessed he needed to do the same for Adam. But first he'd get Adam to the embassy and get the ball rolling on the new passport. Maybe hold off the big reveal for a few days and simply enjoy the other man's company for a while. Two weeks was a long time stuck in each other's company otherwise.

THE WALK BACK TO HIS CABIN WAS FILLED WITH FAR TOO much thinking, and Scott wasn't sure he could really ignore the message for the two full weeks. He should never have read the damn thing. Shame hindsight was such a bitch. He could have been blissfully unaware and not had this nagging little voice in his head telling him he was being taken for a fool all over again.

Shut up! The little voice gave him an indignant snort before disappearing. Entering his cabin, he was hit by a humid cloud of sweet-smelling shampoo. His shampoo. He stopped in the doorway and looked to where Adam was sitting on the bed. Adam was dressed in his clothes from yesterday, and his hair was fluffy and damp from having a shower.

"Hi," Adam said and was quickly on his feet and bounding toward Scott. He practically flung himself at Scott and wrapped his arms around his neck, planting a firm kiss to his mouth.

"What was that for?" Scott said. He rested his hands on Adam's slim waist and looked into his deep brown eyes. In that moment, he reassured himself that Adam wouldn't lie to him. He was being an idiot, doubting Adam when there was no need to.

"Because I missed you," Adam said and grinned.

"What time is it?" He pressed his body to Scott's and kissed him again.

"Just before nine. I thought we could head out now. Maybe get something for lunch afterward."

Adam smiled brightly. "That would be good." He didn't look like a man keeping secrets. "We could talk some more." But apparently, there were still things for him to say.

Scott hugged Adam tight. *Please don't let either of us ruin this. I only just got him back.* "Sure. We can do that." He closed his eyes and breathed in the scent of his own shampoo. Old memories came to the surface, and he just hoped history didn't repeat itself. He wasn't sure his heart could take it all over again.

Chapter Eleven

The *Liberty* bumped the dock, and Scott jumped off to tie her up. He pocketed the keys, then waited for Adam to join him on the dock. Nassau had a very different feel than Marsh Harbor. Big luxury yachts fought for space with smaller cruise boats for hire, and the mix of tourists and locals was enough to make the marina area busy and noisy. Just off the coast several huge cruise ships sat idle, obviously waiting for the return of passengers before setting off on the next leg of the journey.

They completed the short paperwork for docking, then passed through the marina area and onto the main road. Scott appeared to know where he was going, and Adam didn't argue when Scott hailed a cab. The heat was intense, and Adam felt the prickle of sweat down his spine. The small car was air-conditioned and for a few brief minutes Adam was cool. They hadn't talked much on the trip over —content to sit and relax and exchange stupid grins every so often.

The time gave him a space to think. Another damn text

had arrived overnight, and he'd deleted it immediately when he woke up. But…what if the text had arrived and Scott read it? He'd know that Adam hadn't cut all ties with his old life. He wasn't getting involved with Bobby and knew he should cut the guy dead. Problem was, he owed Maury, but would Maury really want him to sacrifice a chance at getting back with Scott?

"We're here," Scott announced as the taxi came to a stop. The embassy building wasn't what he was expecting —not as ornate as some of the other places they had driven past, but he hoped to hell it had air-conditioning as well. They got through security and then had a half-hour wait to see someone, so they made themselves comfortable with cold drinks and magazines.

"Why do I feel guilty?" Adam murmured.

Scott chuckled. "It's like waiting for the principal at school."

Adam thumbed through the magazine he'd picked up and was past halfway before realizing he was simply flicking and not reading at all.

Scott placed a hand on his thigh. "There's nothing to be worried about," he said.

"Easy for you to say," Adam said tiredly. "They'll ask all these questions."

"About your record." Scott turned a little in his seat and used a finger to Adam's chin to get him to meet his gaze. Adam considered fighting it and not having that intimate connection. The text he'd received burned in his head, and he felt guilty. "There's nothing to worry about. We'll go in, get this done, get lunch."

"I have things I want to tell you," Adam said.

Important things that mean we won't have any lies between us.

"I'll be listening."

"Mr Adam Ross?" A tall, thin woman with a ready smile called his name, and with a deep breath Adam stood. Scott didn't move immediately and even though he'd said he wanted to come in with Adam, he was evidently waiting to be asked. Adam held out a hand and Scott took it as he stood. Together they followed the woman into the room. Together was comforting and normal…and good.

THEY LEFT THE EMBASSY AFTER NINETY MINUTES OF FORM filling and questions. Adam had to tick boxes for ethnicity, gender, criminal prosecution. Ms Nesbitt, as they learned her name was, didn't bat an eyelid. She signed off on everything, took his cell number and the number for Sapphire Cay, and when Adam stepped out into the wall of heat that was Nassau, he felt like the weight on his shoulders had eased a little.

"Where do you want to eat?" Scott asked. They were holding hands again and Adam loved the connection. No one stared at them really, they were just a normal couple slowly being roasted alive by the afternoon sun.

"I know somewhere," Adam said hesitantly. "I saw a sign and it's a place I read about…"

"Show the way," Scott replied instantly.

Adam waited a moment and got his bearings. He recalled the sign for Sampson's from the taxi and decided the place couldn't be more than a few minutes' walk.

Sticking close to the buildings for the shade, they made it to the tiny restaurant stuck between a fast food chain and a Ferrari dealership. Nassau was a place full of contradictions. They managed to get a table—one of many small tables set in such a way that the atmosphere was cozy and private.

"They serve the best Cracked Conch here," Adam said enthusiastically. Then he dipped his gaze when Scott smiled.

"They do?" Scott placed his menu on the table. "You order for me."

"You're sure?"

"You know your stuff," Scott pointed out.

Orders taken, the two men were left in the secluded corner sipping a fruity concoction of wine and sangria. Scott only took one glass.

"You don't want to end up in Miami," he smirked. "Unless you want to pilot *Liberty*."

"Pilot Dylan's baby? Nuh-uh." Adam laid his hand flat on the table within Scott's reach and relaxed immediately when Scott laced his fingers with his. For a while they sat discussing anything and everything but not once focusing on anything in particular, until finally it appeared Scott wanted to hear what Adam had to say.

"So, you wanted to talk?" Scott prompted gently.

Adam blanked. His thoughts buzzed inside him. Then with determination, he placed his drink on the table then rooted around in his pocket for his cell. He placed it flat on the table between them, and Scott glanced down at it curiously.

"I got a text. Well three, actually."

"Okay." Scott tightened his grip on Adam's hand briefly. Was he tense? Or was that a gesture of support?

"A guy who I used to run with, way back…" Adam's words failed him.

"When you stole cars," Scott encouraged gently.

Adam dipped his head. "Yeah, the guy who texted, his brother was good to me, he helped me after I came out of prison. I owe him. The brother I mean. Maury his name is. I don't owe Bobby, that was the guy who I used to…you know…" He paused again, then looked up to see Scott impassive and quiet. "I don't know how to explain it," he finished weakly.

"What was the text about?"

"A Nissan GT-R," Adam blurted. He immediately regretted the explosion when Scott narrowed his expression.

"To steal?"

"Maury asked me to be nice to Bobby, to look out for him. I mean, it worked for me, right? Having a mentor, or at least someone to help you, it helps. I realized what I had lost in you, understood I had fucked up my entire life. I thought, and so did Maury, that if we could get Bobby to see what he could lose, to see there was another way, then he could make something of himself. But…" Adam shrugged.

"It didn't work," Scott finished helpfully.

"He's still looking for that easy way out. And who am I to judge him for that? Hell, it's what I did. He has a car, the GT-R, I used to be able to get in the older Skylines in less than a minute. I could, I mean. He wants me to work with him. I deleted the first text, then when I saw he'd sent me another message I turned the phone off. Then last night he texted me again. Here. You can read them. I didn't reply." One-handed, Adam forwarded through his texts and turned the phone to face Scott. They still held hands and Scott hadn't made an effort to pull the grip apart. Scott reached for the phone, and in a very deliberate move, he turned it facedown.

"Tell me about the Cracked Conch, what makes it so special?" Scott asked. Adam was disconcerted. Did Scott not want to read the texts? Or ask questions?

"Seriously?" Adam said, bewildered. "I tell you my past is reaching out to me and you want to talk about the Cracked Conch?"

"It's what you do," Scott pointed out. "You. Adam Ross. You're a chef with a bright future, and you have a man who loves you and wants to be part of that future."

Adam didn't know what to address first in all of that. "But the texts?"

"The texts are your past. Our past. I'm sure that you'll tell this Maury guy that you need to talk about his brother, find another way to help him."

"Just like that. You know I'll do that, and you don't have any doubts?"

Scott smiled and leaned over to place a gentle kiss on Adam's lips. "None."

The waiter arrived with the Cracked Conch and thick wedges of lime, and Adam was happy for the interruption. Scott didn't ask for explanations. He just accepted that Adam would do the right thing and that he trusted him. The heavy weight of guilt and secrets lifted an ounce at a time until, when the Conch was finished and they waited for dessert, Adam felt like a different man.

The journey back to Sapphire Cay was like the first steps into a new life for Adam. A life filled with so many possibilities that he was dizzy from it all.

"How long do you have left in school?" Scott asked from his perch at the wheel. Adam stretched and turned his face up to the waning early evening sun. He delayed answering to give the impression that he had to add up the days when in fact he knew exactly how long until he received his certification.

"Two months," he rounded up.

"Are you pleased to be this close to finishing?"

Pleased? Terrified more like. Getting into the course was easy enough, surviving the three years was okay, but getting a job with a black mark against his name? That was something else.

"Yes," he lied quickly.

"Dylan caught me in the kitchens at the Cay. Dominiq is close to retiring and could use someone to help. He'd been in and talked to Dylan already about offering you a training position. The gig is only for six months a year and the pay isn't earth shattering, but there is a cabin we can share and food as well. For a few seasons maybe, until you have the experience under your belt."

"What do you do for the other six months?"

"Travel. Visit family. Dylan said he'd give you a chance."

"He doesn't know me," Adam protested immediately.

Scott shrugged then smiled broadly. "Dominiq does.

He's told Dylan what you are capable of, the skills you have, and that is good enough for him and Lucas."

Adam felt as wired as a kid at Christmas. This could be a good life laid in front of him. A training position, a beautiful Cay in the middle of sapphire seas, the chance to travel, and above all, Scott.

The *Liberty* bumped the small dock on the beach. Adam didn't even realize they had reached home. Scott tied off the boat and Adam helped. Together they walked up the beach holding hands.

"We have mojitos," Lucas called from the bar and held up a vivid orange drink. Dylan and Dominiq were sprawled on the sand and seemed a little worse for drink. They sure appeared to be enjoying having no guests. Adam tugged Scott's hand. He wasn't part of this group yet and was happy to go back to his room—Scott would find him later, he was sure of it. Only Scott didn't let go of his hand. If anything, he tightened his grip and dragged Adam to the bar on the patio by the pool. He pulled Adam down until they joined the group as Lucas haphazardly delivered a tray of drinks.

"How was Nassau?" Dominiq asked.

"Hot, noisy, too many tourists," Scott deadpanned.

"Big," Adam added.

Dylan shuffled closer to Lucas and leaned on him. They were so easy together, like he and Scott had been before and how he wanted them to be again.

Lucas wrapped an arm around Dylan's shoulder. "Did you manage to arrange for a new passport?"

"It was a lot of form filling and ticking boxes." Adam

played down the fact he had been worried even though he knew Dominiq would understand.

"Did Scott ask you about the kitchen position?"

Adam nodded. "If you're sure…" He looked from Dylan to Lucas then to Dominiq.

"Get your certification," Dominiq said gruffly. "Come back. You're good."

Scott lifted his arm around Adam's shoulder, held him firmly until he finally relaxed into the support. He listened as the others laughed about something to do with weddings and gazebos. He felt Scott kiss a small trail on his neck, then his lips were at Adam's ear.

"I love you," Scott said softly.

With a smile of contentment Adam wriggled closer.

Everything was possible now.

Chapter Twelve

ADAM LOOKED THOUGHTFULLY AT THE SCREEN OF HIS phone. He eyed the quarter-full battery symbol and chewed on his lip. He could just let it run down completely, cut himself off from everywhere and everyone apart from Sapphire Cay and Scott. Sounded kind of nice—just him and Scott and the wide-open space of the ocean. But that was a ridiculous idea. Picking up the sealed plastic bag, he tore at the transparent polyethylene. While in Nassau, he and Scott had found a secondhand electrical store. To Adam's mind it had looked almost as shady as he'd once been, but Scott had seemed perfectly fine with it, asking after a charger so Adam could return the one he'd borrowed from Dylan.

There was no way it was an official charger, more like something you could pick up off eBay for ten bucks, but it would do the job. Plugging in his cell, he rested the phone on the dresser. He'd give it a couple of hours before making the call he needed to. Hell, if it was down to him, he'd probably leave it a couple of months, years even.

"You ready?" Scott asked as his head appeared in the gap of the open door. He grinned as he pushed the door open a little farther and stepped inside. "We're fueled and ready to go if you think you can keep up."

"I'll be just fine," Adam said and turned his back on Scott. "Zip me up." Closing his eyes, he enjoyed the feel of Scott being close, his hands running up Adam's back and then drawing up the zipper.

"You could have done it yourself," Scott whispered at his ear. He tugged at the cord attached to the wetsuit's zipper. "That's what this is for." He tugged again to make his point.

Adam looked over his shoulder. "I like it when you do it." He leaned back against Scott's firm body and smiled as Scott circled his waist with his arms. He felt safe and comforted knowing Scott was there. That feeling was something he never wanted to lose—couldn't.

Kissing Adam's cheek, Scott released his hold. "Come on," he said and took Adam by the hand, guiding him to the door and outside.

The afternoon sun was gloriously bright as Adam stepped outside, and the feel of it against his skin was warming. His heart beat firmly in his chest as he looked at Scott and Scott looked back at him. He was happier than he ever thought possible. He let Scott lead the way, taking him down past the hotel and toward the beach and jetty. They walked hand in hand across the sand and then along the pier, stopping beside the *Liberty*. On the opposite side of the boardwalk from the reliable old boat, two jet skis were moored.

"These things safe?" Adam asked. From what Scott

had said they were brand new, one of Dylan's recent purchases to entertain honeymooners and vacationers.

"Perfectly," Scott said. "Unless you scratch the paint. Then you might want to give Dylan a wide berth for a little while, or you may find yourself on the end of a fishing line being used as shark bait."

Adam nodded and then suddenly stopped. "Wait, sharks?" He eyed the calm sea and folded his arms across his chest.

Scott laughed. "You and sharks. It was a joke…kind of. He'd have to take you way out to use you for shark bait." He rested his hand on Adam's shoulder. "Besides, I'm here to keep you safe."

Adam relaxed and headed for the first of the jet skis, a bright red Kawasaki. "How fast do these go?" He carefully stepped across the gap between the jetty and the jet ski and slid onto the seat.

"Seventy plus," Scott said, taking his seat on the second jet ski. "You still like things fast?" There was a touch of innuendo in his voice.

Not giving Scott an answer, he turned the key of the ski and grinned at the vibration between his thighs. Untying the guide rope, he pushed away from the side of the pier. "Reef's about a half mile out, right?" he checked. Last thing he wanted was to wedge himself in some coral.

"Yep," Scott said as he fastened his life vest. He'd given Adam a thorough safety talk during breakfast.

Adam revved the engine and grinned. "Let's see who needs to keep up with whom," he said. Before Scott could say anything else, Adam accelerated and was away, water spraying high in the air behind him as he sped forward.

The warm breeze hit his face accompanied by a cooling spray of salty water as the ski bobbed and weaved through the waves. The feeling of freedom was exhilarating, and Adam dared to close his eyes—just for a moment. A single perfect moment. Everything from before was forgotten. This last week he'd been the man Scott deserved. No stealing, no going behind Scott's back, no cops and prison, just being normal, together, a couple in love.

Opening his eyes, Adam looked over his shoulder and smiled as he caught sight of Scott against the haze of the bright sun, the two of them separated by a cascading rainbow created from the spray of the jet ski. This was what he wanted. He'd finish college and take Dylan up on the offer of working at the hotel. He'd travel in the off-season if that's what Scott wanted, anything. He wanted Scott to be happy, and hell, it was time to have a little happiness for himself too. Once they returned to the cabin, he'd call Maury and say what he needed to. The past was the past and that was where it was going to stay.

THE DAY HAD GOTTEN AWAY FROM HIM, AND BEFORE HE knew it, the sun was setting, and he found himself alone on the beach watching the light dip below the line of the ocean. Frowning, he looked down at his fully charged phone. He'd put off calling Maury all day, instead enjoying the time he'd had with Scott. The time in the cabin, in bed, mapping out every tanned line of each other's bodies and the time they'd spent on the beach lying hand in hand as they discussed possibilities for the future—their future. For that to truly be an option, he needed to call Maury. He needed to sever the one tie binding him to his old life.

"You okay?"

Adam jumped as Scott spoke and rested his hand on his shoulder.

"Adam?"

Adam nodded. "I'm fine," he assured Scott and smiled as Scott sat beside him on the sand. He was just finding it harder than he thought to call Maury and tell him he could have nothing more to do with Bobby. Not until Bobby changed his ways. As much as Maury thought Adam could be the one to do that, in truth, Bobby needed to find his own reasons for leaving behind the way of life he'd grown accustomed to. He had to take those first steps, and he had to want to change.

"You don't look fine." Scott reached out and wrapped his hand around Adam's, in which he held his cell phone. "You don't have to do it now."

"No," Adam said. "I do." He looked into Scott's eyes and nodded with each word. "I do."

Scott wrapped his other arm around Adam's shoulder and pulled him into a hug. "Do you want me to go?"

Did he? Adam closed his eyes and breathed in the scent of his lover. The smell of citrus and the island warmed him through from head to toe. "No," he decided. "Don't go." It would be easier if Scott stayed. A very definite reminder of why he was doing this.

Scott tightened his hug for a moment and then released Adam. "I'll be here."

Adam shifted on the sand and twisted slightly away from Scott. Adam would really rather be anywhere but here. With a heavy sigh, he made the call, his palm sweating around the case of his cell as he waited on Maury to pick up.

"Hello," Maury said as he answered, accompanied with a strange sound as he seemed to clear his throat.

"Hey," replied Adam. Despite having the conversation running over and over in his head for the last hour, words seemed to fail him now it came down to it.

"'S'up?" Maury asked. "I was just about to put the girls to bed."

"How is everyone?" Good. Conversation. Avoidance. This was good—Adam liked avoidance.

"We're good. You?"

Glancing over his shoulder, Adam's gaze fell to Scott's hands. He smiled as he watched Scott sift white sand from one hand to the other and back again. "I'm great, actually," he said as Scott looked at him and smiled. Returning the smile, he then stared back out at the ocean.

"You found what you were looking for?"

He had and it was so much bigger and better than he could ever have imagined. "I need to talk to you. I need to talk about Bobby."

The silence that followed left a bitter taste in the back of Adam's throat. What must Maury think of him? They'd been friends for years and had always looked out for each other.

"How is Scott?" Maury asked instead.

"Maury—"

"He took you back. Despite everything, he took you back, right?" If he was trying to make Adam feel guilty then it was working. Yes, Scott had forgiven him and somehow they had managed to work things out and pick up pretty much from where they'd left off. Was he supposed to do the same for Bobby? Was that what Maury was implying? Was he supposed to let Bobby back into his life?

Maury made a thoughtful sound, what seemed to be a click of his mouth before he spoke again. "Then let me worry about Bobby."

Adam didn't know what to say.

"I know about the texts. About the car."

Adam closed his eyes. *Shit*. Bobby had never been good at keeping his mouth shut. Always playing the big I am and mouthing off to the wrong people, usually after a beer or five. "I'm sorry."

"It's not your problem."

"It shouldn't be yours either." Maury had his own life —a wife, kids, a mortgage. He shouldn't be getting mixed up in Bobby's business any more than Adam should.

He could imagine Maury smiling on the other end of the phone as he said, "He's my brother. Sure, he's an idiot, but he's my brother."

Regret pained through him. "I wish I could help him. I really do."

"Don't beat yourself up about it. I'm proud of you."

Warmth spread through Adam's chest at Maury's words. The more mature of the twins, Maury had always taken on a big brother role for him and Bobby. "Thank you."

"Don't worry about Bobby." *Easier said than done*, Adam figured. "You do what's right for you. Let me worry about him."

"I really am sorry," Adam said. He closed his eyes as Scott rested his hand on his back. He appreciated the support of his lover and listened as Maury made his reasons to end the call.

"The girls want their bedtime story. Call me when you're back in town. We should get a drink."

Adam smiled. "Okay. I'll call you."

"Night, Adam."

"Yeah, night."

AS ADAM ENDED THE CALL, SCOTT FELT THE TENSION leave his lover's body. He knew Adam had been worried about contacting Maury. The two men had been friends since Scott remembered, Bobby too, and as close as any brothers.

"You okay?" Scott asked and squeezed Adam's shoulder. He wasn't sure what else to say. They both knew cutting Bobby out of Adam's life was for the best—the removal of temptation. Adam wanted to be better and succeed in a career, not go back to boosting cars and watching his back. Scott knew that and he wanted to be as supportive as he could. He didn't have much money of his own, but he had enough to support himself and Adam if he needed to. He wouldn't let Adam fail.

Adam sighed and leaned back into Scott's hold. "I'm good. Maury was okay with everything. He's going to talk to Bobby."

"Good," Scott said with a nod of his head. So, this was it, just the two of them. Only each other to blame if things went to shit between them again. He looked down at Adam and smiled. They'd be just fine.

"Do you remember when we met?" Adam suddenly asked.

Scott wrapped his arms around Adam as they both looked out toward the water. "Yeah," he said. He remembered it and had often wished they'd never met in the years he'd been nursing his broken heart.

"What do you think our lives would have been if we hadn't been at that party?"

Scott rested his chin on top of Adam's head and pressed his chest to Adam's back. He could see the barely legal Adam now, nineteen, skinny, charming. If he hadn't been drinking, Scott doubted he'd ever have had the courage to walk over there after their eyes had met for a third time. "It doesn't matter. We can't change the past."

"But what if?"

Scott lifted his head and leaned forward, capturing Adam's mouth in a brief kiss. "It doesn't matter, and you know why?"

Adam looked up at him, all doe-eyed and curious.

"Because I wouldn't change here and now for anything. I love you, Adam Ross, and if it's okay by you, I'd like to love you for a long, long time." He didn't care if he sounded like some romantic fool. He was the happiest he'd been in a long time. He had never really gotten over Adam. The way he figured, there had always been a part of his heart that loved Adam and would probably never stop loving him, no matter what happened in the future.

Twisting around, Adam wrapped his arms around Scott's neck. "I think I could live with that," he said and pulled himself close. He ghosted his mouth against Scott's in a light kiss, gently mapping out the curve of Scott's lips as if they were new to him.

His dick hardened in his pants, and Scott could barely stop himself from pushing Adam down to the sand and stripping the guy bare. They'd already had sex twice that afternoon, losing it in each other's arms as they kissed and touched and fucked. God, what Adam did to him. Suppressing the overwhelming urge to manhandle Adam out of his clothes, Scott cupped his lover's face and deepened the kiss, his tongue seeking out the warm, wet cavern of Adam's mouth. He loved this man and he had no idea how he would handle it when the time came for Adam to head back home, but he would have to. Adam needed to go home, graduate, take steps for his future. Their future. Scott broke the kiss and wrapped Adam in a hug.

"I love you," he said.

"I love you too."

Epilogue

SCOTT WOKE WITH A START. THE ROOM WAS FILLED WITH light and with absolute certainty he knew he had slept through the night. A glance at his bedside clock showed it was a little after ten am. Luxury. He stretched and only stopped when his hand met flesh.

Adam softly snored next to him, and in sleep he was no longer the quick always-on-the-move guy that Scott was learning more about each day. His brown hair was mussed and some of it sticking in all directions, and his two-day stubble highlighted his slim face. He'd been just as tired as Scott. Work on the catering for the Dawson wedding had been all hands on deck with Edward cracking orders at every turn.

Scott peered closely at Adam's face. He looked healthier now—his skin was sun-brown and his face had filled out a little. They'd been together, here at Sapphire Cay, for a whole month. Adam had passed his course, got his certificates, and arrived at the Cay as soon as he was

132 · RJ SCOTT & MEREDITH RUSSELL

able. Two months apart had been maddening, frustrating, and so long.

Shuffling in bed and realigning covers, he cuddled up to Adam and inhaled the scent of him. When Adam had stumbled in, red eyed from peeling onions and stinking of garlic, he'd taken a shower before coming to bed. This morning he still smelled of lemon and just that single sense memory had Scott wanting a taste. He was already hard. They hadn't made love last night—both too tired to do any more than fall into bed, Adam's hair still wet and his naked skin damp.

Scott traced a path with his lips from one nipple to the next, then blew on the skin and watched it pucker. Adam could get off on just having his nipples sucked and bitten, and Scott loved the way his lover squirmed under him.

"Mornin'," Adam murmured. He yawned and in the same moment arched up into Scott's touch.

"Wanna?" Scott said softly. He moved down from nipples to navel and spent a long time kissing hipbones before being presented with the prize he wanted. Adam was hard and needy and so damn pretty. Scott crawled until he straddled Adam's knees, then concentrated on the weight and texture and taste of his lover. He leaned forward and swallowed Adam as far as he could, using his hand to cover from lips to the base of Adam's cock.

"Wh-what a w-way to wake up," Adam said on a groan. From the delicious sounds he was making and the way Adam moved in a sinuous rhythm, Scott could tell Adam was close. Gripping Adam's hipbones, Scott held him still as he sucked more of the length in then released the suck with a broad sweep of his tongue from root to tip.

Adam reached down and curled his fingers into Scott's soft hair, and with a curse he was coming down Scott's throat. Scott smiled around the orgasm and backed off, wiping his wet mouth as he did.

"I want inside," he demanded.

Adam, still lost in the bliss of orgasm, reached blindly for the ever-present lube on the bedside table and cursed until he had his fingers around the tube. Squeezing out way more than was needed, Adam spread his legs and curled his upper body to reach between them. They had done this so many times. Scott got off on watching Adam stretch himself, on hearing the filthy words and noises coming from Adam's mouth. Quietly, he observed— permanently close to the edge with Adam. Always. His lover, so pretty writhing on his own fingers, was a picture he would carry with him forever.

Impatient to be inside, Scott sheathed himself and in an unspoken plea, he moved between Adam's legs and pushed his lover's hands aside. Adam simply gripped under his own knees and rocked up, waiting for Scott. In a second Scott was inside and so strong, and suddenly he was close to losing it.

He pushed deep inside, the press and retreat almost too much. He wasn't sure how close Adam was, whether or not his lover would come like this again, but he angled until he pegged the gland inside of Adam, and abruptly, Adam was way more vocal. He closed his eyes and his mouth fell open on a moan. Scott curled over and leaned forward to kiss and in a few more strokes he was lost as his orgasm swept through him.

"I love you," he breathed. Pushing forward he closed a

hand around Adam's cock and set up a counter-rhythm. In no more than a few seconds, Adam was coming again. The stamina of his young lover was amazing.

Scott pulled out and flopped to one side, completely drained and sleepy again.

"Not bad for an old man," Adam teased. It was as if he could read Scott's thoughts. Scott was only three years older than Adam, but hell if he could manage two orgasms in a row as well as Adam could.

"What's the time?" Adam asked sleepily.

"Not time to get up yet."

They cuddled close under the lazily moving ceiling fan. "You realize Edward will come find us if we're not out soon."

"Dominiq said I'm not needed until midday," Adam protested.

The knock on the door was loud and strong.

"Guys, up and at 'em. Edward needs us on light-stringing duty."

"Great," Scott groaned under his breath. "He's sent Jamie to do his dirty work."

"I can take Jamie," Adam said quietly, then laughed softly.

"You think you can take an ex-Marine on?"

"Easy."

"What will you do? Kill him with a cucumber?"

"Did you not know I had mad ninja skills with all kinds of kitchen produce?"

The two men grinned at each other.

"Guys!" Jamie shouted again with another knock.

"We'll be there in twenty," Scott called.

Jamie snorted. "Make it five or I'm sending Edward in himself."

They heard his footsteps retreating and had one final hug before rolling out of bed and into the shower, which they kind of shared and which kind of got just a little hot and heavy.

When they entered the large room with boxes open on the floor, they stopped in front of Edward, who simply stared at them with disapproval.

"Told you so," Jamie sing-songed from behind them.

Edward shot Jamie a look, then melted when Jamie blew him a kiss. Then he turned to Scott and Adam. "Scott, you take blue, Adam, pink, and for God's sake don't mix the two."

Adam collected his box, as did Scott, and soon they were busy linking the tiny lights in strings around the room. Adam worked one way, Scott the other, and inevitably they met in the middle.

The kiss was searing and perfect and the *I love yous* gentle and heartfelt.

"Maybe one day this will all be for us," Adam whispered.

Scott glanced at the blue lights in his hand. "Really? You'd want to?"

"Spend the rest of my life with the man I love as my husband? Why wouldn't I?"

They kissed again. Scott's head was spinning with ideas—he could maybe propose in the gazebo next season on a beautiful balmy night, and they could seal all of this officially.

"What are you thinking about?" Adam teased.

Scott smiled. "You," he began quietly. "Always you."

Read the next book in Sapphire Cay - Christmas in the Sun

Christmas is a time for family on Sapphire Cay, but forgiveness is difficult to give and sometimes even harder to receive.

Lucas and Dylan invite their friends to share in their Christmas celebrations on the island along with Lucas's sister, Tasha, and her husband. Christmas is a time for family, forgiveness, and looking to the future, and this year Dylan has to face all three ghosts.

Unearthing the memories of two men in love, frozen in time and buried among the island's history, Lucas and Dylan realize that sometimes loving someone is not always enough. It's about being brave and taking the next step, to learn from the past to move forward.

Family has always been important to Lucas since his own was destroyed by tragedy. Though Dylan disapproves of his methods, Lucas has nothing but good intentions about wanting Dylan to reconcile with his father. The two Gray men haven't spoken properly in years, their relationship strained by heartache and mistakes reaching back into Dylan's childhood.

Boyfriends for Hire

Boyfriends For Hire

1. <u>Darcy</u>
2. <u>Kaden</u>
3. Gideon
4. Jared
5. Felix
6. Caleb

Standalone Christmas

- <u>The Road to Frosty Hollow</u>

Also from RJ & Meredith

Standalone Christmas

- <u>The Road to Frosty Hollow</u>

Free Reads

- Stronger Together

Meet RJ Scott

RJ discovered romance in books at a very young age and realized that if there wasn't romance on the page, she could create it in her head. With over one hundred and fifty books published, she is a full time author of gay romance.

She lives and works out of her home in the beautiful English countryside, spends her spare time reading, watching films, and enjoying time with her family.

The last time she had a week's break from writing she didn't like it one little bit and has yet to meet a box of chocolates she couldn't defeat.

www.rjscott.co.uk | rj@rjscott.co.uk

NEWSLETTER - rjscott.co.uk/rjnews

facebook.com/author.rjscott

instagram.com/rjscott_author

amazon.com/author/rj-scott

bookbub.com/authors/rj-scott

goodreads.com/rjscott

patreon.com/RJScott

Meet Meredith Russell

Meredith Russell lives in the heart of England. An avid fan of many story genres, she enjoys nothing less than a happy ending. She believes in heroes and romance and strives to reflect this in her writing. Sharing her imagination and passion for stories and characters is a dream Meredith is excited to turn into reality.

www.meredithrussell.co.uk
meredithrussell666@gmail.com

 facebook.com/meredithrussellauthor
 x.com/MeredithRAuthor
 instagram.com/miss_meredith_r